THE PLACE OF THE CHINS

In 1944, Scoop Britwell, British war correspondent, is to be dropped into Burma along with a deployment of commandos, back-up for the fighting, forgotten army. However, a premature crash landing plunges him into the jungle war with the Japanese. Events push him into an heroic role, endearing him to his commando comrades and the loyal Burmese. And when harsh conditions hold back his despatches, there are many willing helpers to his cause at the Place of the Chins.

Books by David Bingley
in the Linford Mystery Library:

LONG RANGE DESERTER
RENDEZVOUS IN RIO
ELUSIVE WITNESS
CARIBBEAN CRISIS

DAVID BINGLEY

THE PLACE OF THE CHINS

Complete and Unabridged

LINFORD
Leicester

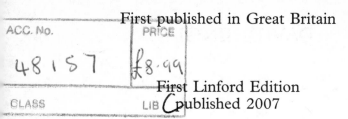
First published in Great Britain

First Linford Edition
published 2007

British Library CIP Data

Bingley, David, *1920 –*
The place of the Chins.—Large print ed.—
Linford mystery library
1. World War, *1939 – 1945*—Burma—Fiction
2. War stories 3. Large type books
I. Title II. Chesham, Henry, *1920 –*
823.9'14 [F]

ISBN 978–1–84782–028–0

Published by
F. A. Thorpe (Publishing)
Anstey, Leicestershire

Set by Words & Graphics Ltd.
Anstey, Leicestershire
Printed and bound in Great Britain by
T. J. International Ltd., Padstow, Cornwall

This book is printed on acid-free paper

1

The time was midnight. The inside of the roomy glider smelled faintly of mules and their droppings. Over a score of damp commandos, men of the 1st Battalion South Lancashire Regiment, part of the spearhead troops of Brigadier Orde Wingate's Chindits, squatted with their backs to the fuselage smoking and talking.

A faint blue light illuminated the formidable soldiers in their sky-drop tunics and protective headgear. The air was full of the accent common to Liverpool. Some wriggled up and peered out through the dirt-grimed portholes, studying the scenes of great activity on the faintly-lit airfield of Lalaghat.

The jump-off airfield for another venture into Burma was located in Assam, the rich tea-growing province which separated the sub-continent of India to the west from Burma, China and

Siam to the east. This was to be more than just a sortie in force. The intention of the C-in-C was to put down his men behind the Japanese lines and build airstrips in patches of lush grassland entirely surrounded by jungle.

Near the partition which separated the passengers from the pilot were two men who felt slightly out of things. They were Harry Britwell, war correspondent of the *Daily Globe* and his partner on this trip, Ronnie Peyton, who belonged to the same newspaper.

Britwell was much the senior in age. In his thirty-seventh year, he had seen action in Norway, on Mediterranean convoys and in Sicily and Italy. For several months he had been desk-bound in London. Now, on the outset of more action for which he had pleaded, he found himself contemplating the future with none of the old excitement and determination which had won for him the reputation envied by many lesser known journalists as 'Our Man at the Front'.

Britwell sat back in his corner with his legs drawn up, contemplating the circling second hand on his luminous wrist watch. Although he had a parachute on his back in addition to his pack, he looked singularly slim compared with the commandos as he had declined a jumping suit and only worn a padded tin hat when the officer of the detachment had insisted. He was dressed in khaki drill with only his shoulder flashes and his tinted green sun spectacles (perched on his forehead) as distinguishing items.

Across from him, twenty-two year old Ronnie Peyton fiddled with the canvas covering case of his precious camera and tried to look at ease. He was a homely-looking youngster nearly as tall as Britwell but a thorough-going lightweight for his height. He was big-boned with a quiff of dark hair sticking out from under his tin hat. His face was kite-shaped. As Britwell stared at him, his wide mobile mouth spread across his face in a toothy grin. His eyesight had kept him out of the forces. He saw the world through slightly-slanted green eyes behind thick lenses in a steel frame.

'Won't be long now, Scoop,' he called

out above the din of conversation, 'the Yankee pilot has just scrambled aboard. He's a sergeant. Looks a bit like John Wayne.'

Britwell shrugged and forced a grin for the other's sake. 'We're in the hands of the military now, Ron. I don't like the look of this crate, but at least it should bring us down again, with luck. One thing I didn't fancy was parachuting, and I find it a relief to be going by glider.'

The older man accepted a piece of chewing gum from his nervous companion and their conversation abated.

Meanwhile, the towing Dakotas continued to taxi up the runway and position themselves ahead of the gliders, which were set out in pairs. Every few minutes one of the American powered craft took off followed by its pair of gliders which bumped and bounced along the grass runway as though reluctant to take-off at all.

Fifteen minutes later, the pilot's partition opened. The full face and thick shoulders of an American sergeant with a crew haircut appeared. He glanced round the squatting soldiers with his eyelids narrowed and his sketchy brows raised.

Sticking up his thumb, he indicated that all was well.

'Won't be long now, you guys! Our tow plane is in position! Hope you Limeys have all written your last will an' testament! Pray for a soft touchdown, all of you!'

A chorus of catcalls from the Liverpudlians made him grin as he closed the door and adjusted himself behind the controls.

The pilot nervously fingered the two rows of medal ribbons neatly sewn to the left side of his tunic as the nylon tow ropes for his own and the sister glider were attached to the tow-ship. The glider men were suddenly aware of revving engines much closer than before. Their Dakota started forward and suddenly the two ropes twitched, writhing like huge serpents until they were taut at full stretch.

The glider jerked forward, the tail lifted and dropped and the craft was being dragged forward like a bucking steer.

Many of the occupants had a feeling they were being pitch-forked into eternity. The disturbing sensation interfered with their digestive systems and several wished that they had eaten more sparingly at the evening meal.

Britwell took the lift-off as badly as any of the others, but his control was good. He withdrew into himself and at once his mind was obsessed with his past troubles.

His last job in the field had been the Italian campaign. A lot of the detail had been given out in his series entitled 'Naples, or Die' which had greatly enhanced his reputation as a graphic writer.

During those rugged weeks when the British and Americans had pushed the Germans northward in the southern half of Italy, he had been a prisoner for a time. Later, he had joined forces with the 3rd Home Counties Commando, of which his brother, Jack, had been an officer.

At a critical time, his brother had been wounded. Tufty, as Jack was known to his cronies, had received a slight head wound at a time when his unit had to take a bridge in difficult circumstances. At that time, moved by the ties of blood, Harry had donned his brother's tunic and led the dicey attack across the bridge. The move had proved successful, but not before the journalist had accounted for one of the opposition.

The remnants of Jack's company had been repatriated after the tricky fighting around the harbour at Naples. Harry had sailed home with them, fully determined to turn over from a non-combatant to a combatant, but there his ambitions had gone awry.

First of all, he had been sent back to his own newspaper in Fleet Street. As he was waiting for a flesh wound to mend on his right hip, he could hardly have done otherwise. Besides, there was still quite a lot of writing to be done upon the heroic series of articles based on the campaign in southern Italy.

The Italian work came to an end about the same time as his doctor signed him off the visiting list. After that, things started to happen. The old editor, Dufrayne, had retired with heart trouble.

A younger man, promoted in wartime to the enviable chair, did not take kindly to his insistence upon turning combatant.

A full Colonel at the War Office seemed to have been warned of his visit. He was put off. The decision, in such circumstances, was not necessarily a military one. At the Ministry of Information, a friend got him an interview with one of the higher ups, a former director of the Globe Publishing Company.

This character, Ralph Hope-Bates, had hinted that he could get a job in the Ministry if he was so keen on a change, but he was very cool when the question of joining the army came up.

'You are too good at your present job, Scoop. Too well known. After that little episode in the Italian action, we can hardly send you back in that theatre of war as a war correspondent, and a voice from the government, perhaps that of the Prime Minister himself, insists that you stay with the *Globe*. So go back to your desk, an' be patient.'

Marisa Perucci, a beautiful charmer of an Italian girl, was behind all his thoughts about returning to Italy and helping to wrest Italian soil from German hands in uniform. Marisa had been his acquaintance of only a few hours, and yet her calm acceptance of wartime conditions, her few dealings with him had warmed his heart more than any other woman had done since his mother. He had promised to seek her out in Battipaglia, a small town south of Naples, at the earliest opportunity.

He had heard nothing of her since that brief forty-eight hour reunion with her behind the fighting line which his bosses had permitted him before shipping him back to UK in a run down condition. A few weeks had gone by before her first letter reached him c/o the *Globe*. Two others followed, at infrequent intervals. Letters full of love and anticipation of a lengthier reunion.

And then had come the one from her father, telling of her untimely death in an air raid. The news had really rocked him, made him rebel against his desk job and clamour to be active again. Hope-Bates and a high ranking army officer friend had put their heads together, and an ultimatum had been delivered to him. He had to stay at a home-based desk permanently, or bury himself for a time in another theatre of war. He had agreed without demur to being sent to the Far East.

He was to be 'buried' in Burma with the Fourteenth Army.

He sighed without knowing it as his hand went towards the shirt pocket where, until just lately, he had kept Marisa's treasured letters. Ronnie Peyton, who was suffering internally himself, heard him groan.

'You all right, Scoop?' he shouted anxiously.

'Eh? Yes, I'm all right, Ron. What made you ask?'

With an effort, Britwell had brought his mind back to the present. To the eerie dull light within the flimsy shell of the glider: to the bucking and yawing motion which had the ebullient stick of commandos fighting a soundless battle with their innards.

'Oh, nothing, really. I thought you

looked a bit under the weather.'

Britwell gave him a reassuring grin and went back to his dismal thoughts.

★   ★   ★

Sergeant Sandy Malone of the United States Army Air Force was not finding his piloting job an easy one.

The veteran Dakota which was towing them had been hard-pressed to raise the two contrary gliders to a height of ten thousand feet in order to top the Chin Hills on their journey east, but it had been done. During the momentous climb the breeze which had assisted their take-off had strengthened.

As soon as the peaks had been cleared, the effort of piloting had been aggravated. On the way up, the gliders had tended to fly wide apart. Now, however, they did the opposite. Every few minutes, the other glider, which contained the officers, a few mules and a signals detachment, came sliding across towards them as though bent upon destroying them.

In avoiding the other craft, Malone

found himself caught time and again in the powerful slipstream of the towing aircraft. In peacetime, he had been a manual worker in a saw mill near Providence, Rhode Island. His work had built him strong arms. They had never been more necessary towards survival than on this son-of-a-bitch of a trip.

Salt sweat ran down his forehead and into his eyes. His shirt was open down the front, revealing more growing sandy hair on his chest than there was on his close-cropped head.

His narrowed eyes had a haunted look in the faintest of reflected light from his instrument panel. His mind was taken up with the tow-ship, the other glider, the tow ropes of both and the razor-like pinnacles of the snow-topped peaks as they slid by beneath him.

He had pinned a picture postcard snapshot of his Italian girl friend who lived in Boston, Massachusetts, to the side of his cockpit. Ever since he took off he had been aware of her, but had never dared to study her dim profile for more than a second. He had to depend upon the mind's eye picture of her to afford himself some relief as he wrestled with the controls like the driver of a roller coaster car which had left the rails.

He started to talk to her. 'Benita, when I told you on that last leave I had all I wanted of medals, I was only spoofin', but right now I mean it. My buddy, Lofty Grout, has charge of the glider next to me, an' if I didn't know him real well I'd think he was pilotin' it to make certain neither of us got back to the States in one piece!

'Here we are, in the dark, over hills not far from the Himalayas an' he comes swingin' at me like a stock car driver aimin' to knock me out of the sky. I swear that if he knocks against my tow-rope I won't know what to do!

'Land's sakes, he'll kill the lot of us for certain sure! What am I talkin' about? Here he comes again, the reckless son of a bitch. Look out, *look out*! The trouble is, I can't tell what he'll do when we swing this close together, if he takes the same sort of avoidin' action I do that'll be curtains for us all!'

13

He groaned as he managed to climb about twenty feet so that the other glider slid away underneath them.

'Benita, you know me, a bit of a bull-shitter on occasion, but I ain't bull-shittin' right now. All I want is to get down in one piece! Anywhere over the United States I'd cut us loose and take the consequences, but here, in the middle of nowhere, with rocky hills and deep rivers an' scores and scores of slanteyes waitin' for us to touch down I wouldn't know how to hit the release button, so help me . . .

'All I ever wanted out of life was to get taken on as a pitcher with Boston Tigers, make a bit of easy money for a few years, sufficient to set you up in a decent house and raise a few kids. You know me, Benita! I'm levellin' with you right now. Oooh.'

Caught in a down-draught, he sucked in breath and set himself afresh to adjust to the new series of problems which the sudden variation was producing. At the same time, there was a knocking on the door to the cockpit. He wanted to yell, 'Come in,' but his voice had gone back on him.

It was a slight relief of sorts when Harry Britwell opened the door, stepped through it and stood with his feet planted apart and his shoulders hunched, peering over his shoulder.

'These air pockets must make manoeuvring very difficult for you!'

Malone dredged up another heart-felt sigh. 'You can say that again, Limey. So help me, I don't know how I've kept us clear of trouble in this past half hour!'

Britwell tapped his shoulder. 'Look out for the other glider, she's homing in on us!'

Malone flinched and murmured, 'Yer, yer.'

He wanted to tell Britwell all about the strains and stresses he had felt since take-off but all his attention was taken up with the manoeuvring. Above all, he did not want to make a bad move in front of this tall Englishman with the correspondent's shoulder flashes.

For a time, Britwell's presence seemed to calm him. The going did not materially ease, but he seemed to cope better and he was glad for a time that the Limey made no attempt to return to the rear.

* * *

Meanwhile, the whole of Ronnie Peyton's nervous system was playing him up. He jumped visibly when Sergeant Dick McCool, the senior NCO of the glider-load of commandos, dug him in the ribs.

'Say, what's the name of your buddy? Is he a flyer by any chance?'

Young Peyton peered closely through his thick spectacles at the sergeant's lined face and puckered brows. He was a man in his thirties, a regular soldier who had been in the fighting from the beginning. The tufts of curly dark brown hair on his cheek-bones fascinated the youthful photographer.

'He's not a flyer, but he's seen plenty of action as a war correspondent. Name of Scoop Britwell. Our Man at the Front. You'll have heard of him.'

McCool had seen and heard enough of the war through personal combat to

16

ignore what the papers said. He had a chronic dislike of non-combatants who came along for the ride.

'A word pedlar, is he? Well I figure we'd have done better bringin' along mules instead of givin' up space to the likes of him!'

This derogatory talk riled the young photographer, who was a fan of Scoop's. In fact, Peyton would not have been on the trip had not Britwell directly intervened on his behalf.

'He may be new to this theatre of war, but he's seen plenty of action! Maybe more than you! He has two thin stripes on his face to show for it and a groove along his right hip. So don't go underestimating him, mister. You'll see what manner of man he is when we get down again!'

McCool wanted to get some more ill-feeling off his chest, but Scoop's reappearance stopped him. The tall reporter leaned down towards them, and pointed back to the cockpit.

'Those air pockets have been giving our American pilot the jitters, but they seem to be easing out a bit now. Don't take a look out, though, it'll make you more sick than ever!'

Scoop resumed his place in the corner with a sardonic grin on his face. As he had predicted, the chasséing of the glider eased off a little as the Chin Hills faded astern.

★　★　★

For an hour, all the passengers achieved a comatose state. Some of them even slept. The Chindwin river was several miles behind them and Scoop was reckoning that they did not have much more than ten miles to go when the bucking and yawing started up all over again, with even greater intensity.

The passengers groaned and began to wake up and take notice. The glider dropped like a lift, leaving them with their hearts in their mouths. Somebody made a bad joke about having to use the parachutes after all and was promptly told to shut his big foolish mouth.

The uncomfortable rising sensation

followed, and then a sudden jar which made the craft do a complete roll in the air. After what seemed an age, it righted itself. Britwell, sensing that something was wrong, scrambled to his feet and re-entered the cockpit. The area smelled of Malone's perspiration. The pilot seemed frozen to the controls as it slipped away to starboard.

He leaned over and slapped the man's cheeks, wondering if he had lost control altogether. Malone partially recovered with saliva pouring from his lips.

'Will you believe that, Limey? This craft is bewitched! Lofty's starboard wing has just fouled our tow line an' I made sure this was to be our coffin, so help me God! I can't take much more of this sort of punishment. You're a decent guy. You can see the punishment I've been taking! What would you do?'

Britwell made a quick assessment of the prevailing conditions.

'You're the pilot, chum. If you think things are going to get worse, and that both gliders are going to crash, as a result, there's only one positive course of action open to you. Hit the release button!'

'Hit the release button?'

Malone turned and peered into his face as if he was off his head.

'If I do that, it means I'll have to make an unaided landing. I'll be working practically blind in this light. How can you say such a thing?'

'It's your responsibility! Remember that two glider loads of dead commandos aren't going to further the war effort very much!'

The tortured pilot caught a glimpse of the sister ship as it commenced on a converging ramming course. He reacted recklessly, kicking over his rudder bar and working his ailerons. The engineless kite clawed its way out of the Dakota's slipstream and banked to starboard once again. The manoeuvre amply avoided the other glider, but Malone seemed slow to react. Britwell braced himself for the pull of the tow rope, but it never came. He was more alert than the pilot. His sharp eyes caught a glimpse of the strands of nylon as they fell away from the tail of the mother ship.

'You're loose!'

Malone stared at the release button, wondering if he had touched it by mistake, or if Britwell had thumbed it while he was not looking.

'Try and relax, mate. The pilot of the tow-ship must have seen the danger we were in. He must have worked some sort of emergency release switch! All you have to do now is put us down as quietly as you can!'

Malone read the signs. The Dakota began to go away from them. So did the other glider. The Limey was right. All he had to do was to put the kite down in one piece. But how was he to do that? No maps, no knowledge of the terrain at all. Jap country, right there below them. It was asking an awful lot.

His fear-raddled face said as much, but Britwell was offering him a swig of rum out of a small flat hip flask.

2

Malone must have swallowed two tots before Britwell managed to wrest the small flask away from his lips. The American had sufficient presence of mind to put the glider on an even keel and then he seemed to go rigid at the controls.

'Pull yourself together, Yank, for all our sakes,' Britwell advised him brusquely. 'You're about twelve thousand feet up and you seem to be heading east. I'd advise you to keep to that direction. The visibility isn't very good with the clouds masking the moon, but you've got time to get over the buffeting you've been having before we hit the deck.

'The choice of landing space will have to be yours. At all events try to miss jungle. The boys back there will be rooting for you when you get down low.'

Malone glanced at him out of his eye corners as he replaced the flask in his hip pocket. 'You goin' back to the others, Limey?'

'Yes, but I'll come back later, if it will help you. Keep her up as long as you can. Give yourself an extended breather.'

So saying, Britwell stepped through the narrow door and closed it after him. He was met by a chorus of protests and queries about their present position and chances.

'The tow plane has cut us loose to prevent a general pile-up,' the Englishman remarked, his gaze fixed on Sergeant McCool.

'I bloody thought as much!' McCool ejaculated. 'That means they've gone on without us. We could be miles away from the landing zone by the time we get down again!'

'Is the Yank capable of putting us down in one piece, Scoop?' Peyton asked, in a curious sounding voice.

'I'd say he knows his job, but the odds are against a smooth landing, Ronnie. All we can do is prepare for the worst and hope for the best!'

The correspondent's reply had carried to the other passengers who appeared to be almost holding their breath. A stocky redheaded commando with a bent nose broke the ensuing silence.

'We do have a choice, lads. What do you think about using the parachutes, sarge? I reckon we've got enough height for a decent drop!'

Dick McCool was slow to answer. 'I figure we ought to stay together, Willie. If we go by parachute, most of us would survive on landing, but we'd be separated. As soon as we touch down, we might come under attack. Besides, we'll have to do what we can to find the rest of our mob who went on to the proper landing zone.' He turned towards Britwell. 'Is he trying to follow the Dakotas?'

'No, I don't think he is, but we can't pressure him. Piloting a glider without a tow-ship is quite different from what he was doing before. There's still quite a bit of breeze, and he'll have to make what use of it he can. All that stuff they taught you at the bush warfare school is going to be put to the test in the near future.'

The commandos relapsed into silence. Peyton burped. Someone else sniffed noisily and one hunched figure groaned.

The tension built up among the passengers. Five minutes crawled by. When Malone thumped on the communicating door everyone reacted sharply.

Britwell rose to his feet again. 'I said I'd go back in there if he wanted any help. I'll let you know as soon as there's any marked development.'

In the cockpit, Malone remarked: 'Hey, Limey, we're down to about five hundred now. I've crossed a couple of ridges, and there's narrow waterways here and there but mostly it's solid stands of timber, what do you make of it?'

Britwell peered over his shoulder. 'It's difficult to be exact about anything in this light. We crossed the Chindwin river some way back. So far as I know there's no other major waterway in this area. Paddy fields look a bit like *chaungs*, because they're often thinly covered with water. If you can't see obvious grassland, head for a stretch of paddy.'

Malone squinted hard ahead of him. 'What's with that word you used? *Chaungs*, did you say?'

'That's right. What do you call them in

the States? They're minor waterways. Creeks, I reckon. The *chaungs* should be fairly deep. Preferable to timber, but this kite is likely to fold up on impact, isn't it? So we don't want to swim unless we have to.'

In spite of himself, Malone began to get back a bit of his old spirit. 'You know, the things you're sayin' aren't givin' me confidence at all, Limey. I like your rum better than I like you, right now. How about another shot?'

Britwell produced his flask. 'All right. One mouthful. I'm going back to the others, then. Give us a knock when you're down to about a hundred feet.'

Malone drank again while the glider slowly lost altitude in dipping loops occasioned by gentle manipulation of the rudder bar and the control column.

'There's a gentle breeze comin' straight at us,' Malone remarked, but Britwell had recovered his flask and removed himself.

'How long, Britwell?' McCool enquired brusquely.

Scoop shrugged. 'I'm no expert. I'd say we'll know the worst within five minutes.'

There was a general shuffling as men experienced in warfare and hard-lying conditions prepared themselves to make the best of a critical situation. Extra weapons, ammunition and other items were lifted down from the bulkheads in an attempt to prevent damage.

The troops were taking the creaks out of their cramped bodies when Malone again thumped on the communicating door. Britwell opened it and left it that way. He felt that the commandos ought to know now what was going on. A brief glance ahead of the glider confirmed that there were no lights, no fires showing in the terrain they were heading for.

'Limey, you got to work for survival. Me, I'm sufferin' from eye strain. You do the lookin', select the landing ground an' I'll work the controls. Okay?'

All kinds of critical words of protest came to his lips, but he did not utter them. 'All right, I'll give it a try!'

A turgid grey *chaung* sailed beneath them in a crosswise direction.

'Take us across it and make sure you clear those trees!'

Malone's breathing sounded almost asthmatic, but he worked on the instructions, skimming over tall trees thickly foliaged at the top with about thirty or forty feet to spare.

'You see anything? You're higher than me, Limey. What can you see, for Christ's sake?'

Britwell, standing with his legs braced in the door frame, suddenly gripped the pilot's left shoulder. He pointed beyond the stand of teak trees to a grey gap about two hundred yards further on.

'There's your landing spot! It's the only possibility that I can see. A clearing of some sort! With a bit of luck it might be a plantation. Whatever it is, steer for it. You don't have enough height to search further!'

Malone muttered: 'We can do with all the luck in the world, and then some.'

Britwell tore himself away from the scene with an effort. Hurriedly, he brought the commandos up to date. In a quieter voice he told young Peyton to brace himself. He was thinking that those near the tail were in a more favourable position, but he did not voice such thoughts.

Only the faint sound of the breeze going past the fuselage reminded them of the continued progress. There was a faint jar like a boat grounding as the glider skimmed the last of the tree tops and converged with the ground. A few seconds of absolute silence were broken by an agonized cry from the pilot.

'It's too short! We're never goin' to make it, I tell you!'

No one argued. All eyes were trained forward, all bodies braced for the jolt of the crash. Malone was in a quandary. If he put the nose down sharply he might just hit the earth before the trees loomed up at the far end of the narrow clearing, but in doing so he stood the risk of killing himself when the cockpit crumpled.

Still upwards of ten feet above the ground, the creaking glider flew past the end of the cleared strip. The port wing caught first. All personnel were thrown forward. Extra packs and two canisters were displaced. They slithered forward along the deck with a grinding noise until they fetched up with the partition.

Abruptly the whole craft, minus about half its port wing, was swung to the left. While men pitched this way and that the craft, nose tilted downwards, collided with another tree bole, this time on the other side. The starboard wing came away with a screech of rending materials. On a few feet precipitately, until another trunk penetrated the flimsy cockpit and brought everything to a standstill.

In the last forward movement, a door in the starboard side of the fuselage had flown open. No fewer than eight soldiers, those seated nearest the tail, bumped and fell through the opening to the earth beneath. The whole area was full of frantic cries and oaths for almost a minute.

Four men crawled clear of the winded bodies of Peyton and Britwell, while Sergeant McCool clawed himself erect and called for order.

'On your feet, you scousers! Out by that starboard door, an' be careful how you go. Could be one or two blokes injured down there! We'll muster as soon as we get clear.'

From a kneeling position, Britwell pointed with his thumb towards the smashed cockpit. 'How about the pilot?'

'Take a look yourself, Britwell, I've got my lads to attend to.'

The sergeant turned away. He started to move towards the door himself, lugging a metal canister behind him. Peyton went through after the last of the commandos rubbing his neck and very conscious of the fact that his spectacle frame was slightly out of line.

'Malone is out cold. He could be dead,' Britwell remarked.

'If he's dead, leave him. Our business is with the livin'. I reckon they paid him danger money for what he did.'

McCool sounded inhuman and Britwell's anxiety turned to anger. 'If he's dead, he died giving us a chance to live, McCool. Maybe you hadn't thought of that!'

The sergeant ignored the retort. Britwell moved gingerly into the cockpit. Malone was crouched forward over the control column with his head tilted downwards. He did not respond when

Britwell touched him lightly on the shoulder. Bits of perspex fell away from his body, which simply slumped lower. There was no pulse at his wrist. A hairy legged spider scrambled round the tree bole just a few inches from the close-cropped head.

Unnoticed by the crash victims, parrots, small birds, monkeys and tiny animals had cried their protest as the glider ploughed into their territory, and then they had gone quiet, having scattered.

Britwell began to haul the body backwards. As he did so, the head swung around on the shoulders with too much freedom for normal. The neck was broken. With an energy-consuming effort, the correspondent fought his way up the fuselage to the door. McCool dropped before he reached it. Left on his own, Scoop manoeuvred Malone's legs through the door and looked down. Only Ronnie Peyton could be seen below, waiting for him.

'All right, step aside and give him room, Ron. He's dead already.'

Britwell felt a bit guilty about the way in which Malone's corpse bounced on arrival, but it could not be helped. Peyton briefly flashed a pencil torch until the last of the packs were grounded. The correspondent then followed, jarring his legs on impact.

'They've gone that way, Scoop. The sergeant headed for a bit of a gully. Said they would use it for a base until daylight. I'll give you a hand with the Yank, if you like.'

There was something troubling Peyton above all else, but it was not until the photographer had stumbled into a part of the gully-like trench and lost his grip on Malone's legs that his partner realized what it was. Britwell had gone down on one knee and nearly followed the corpse into the trench.

'Leave 'im there, Britwell for the time bein',' McCool called. 'I'd like it if you'd come along with me and look over the injured.'

Scoop backtracked about ten yards, armed with the torch. The sergeant took him by the arm and led him to where six men were stretched out between the trees, minus their jumping smocks and helmets. Britwell bent over them in turn. When he had examined no less than three and found them all dead, he turned to McCool with an enquiring look.

'You said injured, Sergeant. I don't want to disappoint you — '

'Yer, yer, I know, troop. We believe they're all dead. Ribs, backs, necks and heads. I'll level with you. I'm not much good with corpses. If my mates are wounded, they usually manage to give me a mouthful of healthy bad language, then I'm all right. It's when they're past talkin' I don't figure so good.'

Britwell continued his inspection, reflecting that the sergeant was human after all. Every one of the six had been killed on impact.

'Do you figure on burying them all before we bed down?'

'No. They'll be doin' their last job to help the livin' tonight. I'll get the boys to plant them around us in a ring. Our six and your pilot. Usually, we leave something by them to make a clatter, in case the enemy tries to creep up on us durin' the night.

'We'll make a barricade of sharpened bamboo sticks as well. Then we get down in the gully. We can light a fire down there without it showin', so we can have tea laced with some of that rum of yours. Things will look brighter by daylight.'

Within half an hour the defensive ring was prepared. The squad hunkered down, drinking tea and talking over the day's events. Two other men had minor injuries. The redhead, Willie More, had slight concussion and another man who answered to the nickname of Everton had wrenched his shoulder.

The night was surprisingly cold after the heat of the day. The survivors were glad of the warmth of the fire as they dropped off to sleep.

★ ★ ★

Mottled sunlight and the cries of tropical birds awakened them at an early hour. Soon they became used to the noise of cicadas and the hums of mosquitoes.

Apes and gibbons, scolding them from a safe distance, ceased to be a novelty as McCool drove his men to bury their dead before breakfast.

The shattered glider was a galling sight to all present and a sure guide to any enemy troops who might be on the lookout for them. The best policy, therefore, was to get clear of the area of the crash as soon as ever possible. No one argued as the bodies were buried in the narrow gully. K-rations were used for breakfast. Presently, the decimated troop formed up. McCool had fourteen fit men under him. Counting the two non-combatants the party amounted to seventeen.

Carrying everything of value, barring the parachutes and jumping smocks, they moved off through the timber in a northerly direction, using wrist compasses to guide them on a route which they hoped would carry them eventually towards the first proposed new airstrip.

In the first hour, the timber thinned out until they were only tramping through teak and high hung lianas. McCool, at the head of the snake column, set a good pace. His fourteen men followed, one behind the other, two or three yards apart. Britwell and Peyton brought up the rear, drinking in the encroaching atmosphere which was new to them both.

In timber, it was easy to forget about vigilance, for the air between the trees had a foetid smell due to excessive heat and damp and the continuous decay of fallen leaves and tendrils underfoot.

Towards mid-morning, the daylight began to filter through the tree tops with greater intensity. Up ahead, it looked as if the teak belt was about to come to an end. McCool, therefore, called a halt in a hollow and permitted the use of fire for the first time in daylight.

The tea tasted good. While they were drinking it, he gave his men a pep talk about looking for items to improve our diet, mentioning pink pumpkin and chillies among other things. He also carried out an inspection of all weapons before moving on again.

Within ten minutes of the restart, the party hit an open patch of muddy ground. The sergeant chose to go east, rather than west around it. In taking that direction, he put his party on a down-hill slope where the foliage was thicker, and by the time they had adjusted to the more difficult going they found themselves on the banks of a low-lying muddy marsh which might have been cultivated as paddy at an earlier time.

From then on, if they wanted to keep going roughly north, it was a matter of following the bank and taking the punishment which the terrain handed out. At first, the troops were careless. Leeches began to drop on them and occasionally large numbers of red ants. There were frequent pauses while a man applied a lighted cigarette to a leech which refused to part from his mate's back or neck.

Previous experience had shown them that a leech left its jaws in the flesh if it was simply pulled away by hand.

For a short distance, they moved along the muddy shallows but the sudden arrival and departure of a couple of fighters with the unmistakable Japanese markings showing sent them scurrying back into cover. The jungle, for the time, was sufficient of an enemy in itself.

Britwell and Peyton soon learned to avoid brushing the trees where the leeches lived, but as their legs grew heavy with tiredness in the early afternoon they pushed through some bushes which McCool described as *bizat*. Their legs were covered in long khaki trousers, but their exposed forearms soon showed blemishes and developed rashes.

The latter pair were discussing this new setback in low tones when Peyton showed anguish for an entirely new reason.

'Scoop, I'll have to mention this. Say I've got too much youthful imagination if you like with all this teeming life around us, but twice in the past half hour I've thought that we were being followed.'

Britwell lifted his sun glasses and studied the younger man's troubled face. 'So *you* had that impression, as well. You could be right. There could be all sorts of everyday explanations, of course, but this is alien country in wartime. I'll pass the word forward.'

He began to snap his thumb and finger in a prearranged way. The man in front began to drop back towards them, his half-closed eyes probing into the trees and bushes at the rear.

3

The finger signal travelled all the way to the leader in very little time. Presently, the message put forward by Britwell had alerted everyone and McCool's immediate reaction was for the others to carry on as usual for a time, except for the journalist who was to move forward and give some further explanation.

Apprehension about the unknown kept the short column moving quite briskly and by the time Britwell caught up with McCool he was slightly out of breath.

'Any further development yet, Britwell?'

'No, none at all. It could be animals, or natives, or even Japs, but if it happened to be the latter I think they would have attempted to get on terms with us before this.'

'Unless they knew we were moving into other units of their forces up ahead,' the sergeant reasoned.

McCool massaged his lined face and tested the dark brown stubble on his chin with a thumb nail. Britwell, who kept pace with him easily enough, slipped one of the webbing straps off his shoulder and swung the pack which contained the radio receiver off his back.

'If it isn't the enemy,' McCool was murmuring, 'we could do more harm than good in merely goin' to earth and openin' up when the followers come along. But we have to get rid of whoever it is, or at least know more about them. Natives in these parts have seen a lot of the Japs lately. They could be pro-Jap or pro-English.'

'I've got an idea, Sergeant. Why don't you look for a place and fake an ordinary camp? Your men could fan out and jump whoever it is without actually shooting.'

McCool sniffed. 'How could we be sure they'd keep comin' after we'd stopped?'

'Lure them on with the radio. Give them a spot of music. Indian music would do. Anything, just about. All you have to do is kid them that we're resting and not on the alert.'

McCool turned and conferred with Mick Judd, a corporal who came from Cheshire. Judd was a short, stocky full-faced individual in his middle twenties with fine brown wavy hair and an unshakable conviction that the men of Cheshire were better soldiers than Lancastrians. He was mild of manner compared with the senior NCO. When asked his opinion of the plan of action, his ill-assorted eyes — one brown and one green in colour — twinkled.

'Give it a try, sarge. Hadn't I better drop to the rear, though, bein' one of the two machine-gunners?'

McCool approved. Judd made his way to the rear, giving the men an inkling as to what was about to happen as he went. Britwell remained at the front and after a short interval, Peyton hurried forward to join him. Fifteen minutes elapsed before McCool found the sort of ground he fancied for the mock camp. There was a natural shelf in the terrain, a drop of three feet before the earth levelled out again.

'This is it, boys,' he remarked. 'The non-combatants will stay here with me.

The rest of you get down out of sight and then split into two groups. Every other man to left and right. I want you to form a couple of crawling pincers until we've encircled whoever it is followin' us. Use your weapons to get control, but don't shoot unless you have to. We can do without gunshots. Now, let's go.'

* * *

As soon as the walking column had split up, excitement and tension mounted. After the hair-raising events in the glider, the pressure had been off the small group. The two Japanese fighters had been the only confirmation that the enemy was anywhere about.

Now, however, it was possible that a clash was imminent. Most soldiers are excitable until a time of crisis, when their professional training and experience enables them to calm down. The music had been blaring out for upwards of five minutes by the time young Peyton got his nerves under control and thought about using his camera for the first time. There was a little less natural light than he would have wished, but he felt justified in trying for a still picture when the mysterious column followers appeared.

Bellied down behind a fallen log, he soon had his apparatus ready. While the minutes dragged by, and an Indian radio station pumped out the sort of popular music approved of by that nation, he had an attack of the jitters. How would it look if the followers were merely one or two boisterous monkeys? Apes, say, or the gibbons of the region?

The non-combatants would surely lose face beyond all reason. He was still oozing with the perspiration brought on by the thoughts of such an embarrassment when he got his first glimpse of a human face. It was no more than a blur, but Scoop had seen it as well as the hard-eyed Dick McCool.

Scoop pretended to be busy with a cooking pot, while McCool toyed with the bolt of his rifle. Seconds later, the intruders had their first inkling that they were surrounded. In a very professional manner, the commandos had done their pincer movement, using the marsh bank and terrain further inland. Now, they rose up behind trees, clicking rifle bolts and generally giving the ambushed characters the idea that they were apprehended.

The first person to step into the open was a nervous Burmese youth with close-cropped black hair and anxious brown eyes set in a young face with a turned down mouth. He was about five-feet six-inches tall in his open sandals. A broad leather belt held in his billowing white trousers and a smock of the same colour. A round coolie hat made out of bamboo strips had slipped to the back of his neck on a cord. His only weapon was a long, flat-bladed jungle knife known as a *dah*, which hung from his belt in a leather sheath.

He raised his hand, as McCool also showed a rifle and started towards him. 'Do not shoot, Sergeant. I know you are English! We are friends of the English!'

Behind him, two other natives had sprung into the open when they realized further hiding behind tree boles had no future. These two had a certain resemblance for each other. They were about ten years older, a few inches taller and heavier by several stones. Their cheekbones and jaws were more pronounced, as were the muscles of their chests and shoulders.

Below the waist, they were similarly clothed to the youth, but above they differed. Their hirsute chests were partially covered by sleeveless unbuttoned waistcoats in dark material. Tightly wound turbans made their bony foreheads seem more pronounced. This latter pair had their *dahs* at the ready, as they stood back to back, but following the first utterance of the youth they lowered the blades and allowed themselves to be loosely herded towards the cooking pot and the fallen tree. At a gesture from McCool they dropped their weapons.

'Every man will stay on the alert until further notice! Get down and keep your weapons handy. Half of you face this way, the others cover us by facin' outwards.'

The trio condescended to kneel.

Peyton, having taken his one picture, was content to look on and listen while Britwell and McCool did the interrogating.

Britwell said: 'For a Burmese, you speak English very well.'

'Friends usually go up and speak to others friends,' McCool began brusquely, 'why did you hang about behind us without makin' yourselves known?'

'We had to be sure first. We came across your trail by accident. Your prints suggested British boots rather than Japanese soldiers' footwear. As you know, our country is full of enemies. We would have overtaken you later, and exchanged informations with you.'

'Who are you, and where do you come from?' Britwell resumed.

'My name is Shan. My friends are Ahmed and Yusuf. They are brothers. We come from a loyal village further east. If you trust us, we could take you there.'

'Soldiers have to go where they are told. If we decide to trust you, we would ask you to take us somewhere else,' McCool put in.

Britwell was impressed by the sergeant's straightforward attempts at interrogation. 'How do you think we got here, Shan?'

For an instant, an uneasy smile flickered over the lad's face.

'From the air, sahib. Where was it you were supposed to go?'

At this point, the other two who also understood English shared the youth's burning curiosity. McCool and Britwell eyed each other and hesitated before divulging what information they had.

Britwell said: 'We have a rendezvous in a flat stretch of grassland situated to the north of two east-west ridges with a narrow passage between. Do you know of such a place?'

The youth frowned. 'Oh, yes, we know such a place, but there are no English soldiers anywhere near there.'

'What is the direction of the grassland from here?' McCool persisted.

The youth shrugged and pointed. 'That way. North. No, north-west, I think. Maybe a day's journey. But why do you want to go there?'

Britwell left this answer to the NCO

who became very thoughtful for a time. 'A good soldier does not give away military information. If we insist upon going to the place my friend has described, we shall expect you to act as our guides. Do you understand?'

Looking troubled, the young Burmese nodded. He got up off his knees and spoke a few sentences to his companions, who answered only in monosyllables, but appeared to agree.

'If you insist, Sergeant, we will guide you, but it would be better if you came to our village straight away.'

The interview was more or less at an end. McCool stood up and relayed the gist of the exchanges to his men. They rose to their feet again and grouped themselves about the fallen tree.

'Have you plenty of water?' Shan asked.

'Is there fresh water near?' McCool asked in his turn.

Shan nodded. There was nothing in the mien of the other two to suggest that he was telling other than the truth. Neither McCool nor Britwell was wholly satisfied with their new 'allies' at this point, but they did need fresh water fairly urgently, and a refilling of the water bottles was likely to ease their problems in the near future.

When the column started out again, Shan, with his *dah* to hand, led the way. The two muscular Burmese were about half way down the line and separated by More and Everton. Britwell and Peyton dropped to the rear again, taking Corporal Judd and his machine-gun with them.

★　★　★

It became clear in the first half hour after the resumption that Shan and his friends knew the local terrain really well. The youth started off in a straight line, not keeping to the edge of the marsh. From time to time, he came upon thick patches of growth, but his *dah* took him through with the minimum of delay.

By mid-afternoon, he announced to McCool that the marsh had come to an end. The sergeant received the news without enthusiasm.

'Don't forget we are supposed to be heading for water. Drinkin' water. The water bottles of some of my men are empty already. A thirsty man does not fight well, let alone travel.'

'Have patience, sahib. All will be well. I am taking you to a place where the water is good, and where your men can bathe, too.'

'How long before we get there?'

'Not much more than an hour, unless we have trouble.'

And with that terse explanation, the NCO had to be satisfied. He supposed that in this land of jungle and other hazards every day on the move and undetected was a victory of sorts. Being a gambler by nature, McCool wondered what the odds were of getting back to the main body without any more reverses. His speculation, however, left him feeling despondent and he desisted.

He had looked at his wrist watch no less than three times in ten minutes when the youthful guide paused five yards ahead of him and pointed accurately through leaning tree trunks ahead and to the right.

The human snake closed up its members, keen with anticipation.

'The *chaung* we have been taking you to is through there. We do not anticipate trouble, but it would be as well if I and my friends went first. You will trust us?'

McCool covered his hesitation by pouring the last few drops of his drinking water over his face. Then he nodded. The trio of natives moved away from them until they reached the leaning trees and there they suddenly dropped out of sight. The Lancastrians slipped off their packs and murmured to one another.

'Don't relax too much yet,' McCool warned. 'Keep your eyes skinned.'

Within a minute one of the older Burmese reappeared and waved his *dah*, gesturing for them to go forward. After warning his men to spread out and go carefully, the NCO led the way. The *chaung* in question was between fifty and a hundred yards wide at the point which they first approached.

The sight of so much moving water

after the rigours of the day put heart in the men. They found the three natives spread around the sides of an inlet which was almost circular in shape.

'Don't go beyond here, please,' Shan advised. 'Give us five minutes before you plunge in.'

The Liverpudlians' patience was scarcely up to the last request, but tempers cooled when they witnessed the next development. The natives slipped off their sandals, rolled up their trousers and slowly waded into the pool. Their concentration was good as they bent double and probed the shallow water with their hands.

Almost at once they started to catch fish and toss them ashore. The commandos ringed the inlet perimeter and reached out to catch them as they were hurled out of the water. Within ten minutes there were fish for everyone. The man known as Everton had his boots and socks off and was running down the slope into the water when Corporal Judd barred his way.

'Water bottles next, sarge?'

McCool nodded. The army issue water canteens were hurled to the paddlers in a great shower. They had scarcely been filled when the bodies of the overheated soldiers plunged into the shallows, scattering the water, and, for a time, the discipline.

The locals were the first to emerge. They collected up the fish and built a fire over which they proceeded to roast the fresh food. The appetizing smell soon began to draw the men ashore again. McCool posted a couple of guards on the inland side and then relaxed.

Some men ate the fish offerings straight away. Others concentrated on boiling water for tea first. Ronnie Peyton rubbed himself down opposite Britwell with a broad grin on his face. He looked like a Boy Scout on his first outing to camp. Not much towelling was necessary. The heat of the day soon began to have its effect again. Britwell wandered from one small group to another, savouring the change in these men who had started the operation badly and been the victims of tension on and off ever since. Everton had forgotten his wrenched shoulder. He was the first to offer a cigarette. Ginger More tossed one over and after that Scoop started to refuse them.

He gradually extracted himself and moved back up the slope. As he exchanged a word here and a joke there, he felt that these clannish soldiers had accepted him as one of themselves. The feeling pleased him immensely, but he steadfastly kept his mind off the future. At this stage, he did not even feel like making notes although that part of his occupation was almost a daily habit with him.

He squatted by himself with his fish, K rations, a mug of tea and a lighted cigarette. Another group apart were the Burmese who had withdrawn to eat, drink and talk. He wondered about their background and what might have happened if the whole party had gone at once to their village, as they had requested.

There was so much activity beside the *chaung* that he omitted for a time to keep an eye on young Peyton. Fifteen minutes went by before it occurred to him to wonder what the young photographer was doing. And then he saw him. Peyton had gone beyond the pool. He was working his way out on a narrow spit of land which protruded into the stream. His shirt tails were flapping outside his trousers. He had his camera gripped tightly in his two hands.

Britwell marvelled at his youthful keenness, and for a time his thoughts were clouded by recollections of all the young men who had fallen around him in the early days of the Italian campaign the preceding year. Peyton poised himself almost unnoticed by the cavorting soldiers and took a photograph. He peered upstream and downstream before setting himself for another. He scowled through his spectacle lenses and was tinkering with the focussing gadget when an unmistakable noise of war broke upon the scene and restored the tension.

It was the sharp, staccato noise of automatic weapons. One fired first from the other side of the *chaung*. Two others joined in. While the commandos crouched and scattered, shouting words of warning to one another, the hapless photographer was caught in the first accurate burst.

His body jerked backwards, appeared to be suspended for a brief second or so and then cavorted this way and that, tossed by the bullets which stitched his trunk. Suddenly he sank down. The air was full of flying lead and vicious oaths.

4

'*Nips across the water!*'

McCool's stentorian voice put into words what every man under his command had already worked out for himself. To the Chindits, the sound of Japanese 'woodpecker' machine guns was nothing new. But for the recklessness of the young photographer, the whole party might have been taken by surprise and decimated, in spite of the watchful Burmese.

There was a sound gap of a few seconds before the machine guns opened up again. This time they were aimed to hit men scrambling away from the pool.

'Grab your kit, keep down an' head away from the water! Chop, chop!'

The sergeant was withdrawing his men. His strategy was sound, as he had no idea of the numbers across the water or how mobile they were. Britwell paused long enough to hook his sun spectacles on his ears and then he was going back to try and help Peyton. No other man went the same way.

He glanced back to see how the others were doing as his booted feet slithered in the shallows.

'Out! Get back, Britwell!' Corporal Judd's voice this time. 'Your mate has bought it! Come away, an' keep down!'

As though to underline Judd's words, a burst of tracer came flying towards the rear slope, chopping down shiny green waterproof leaves and hacking bushes into small pieces. Britwell saw the foolhardiness of his move and began to withdraw. An inch above his scalp, a bullet whipped off his shapeless bush hat and made him suddenly angry.

He went up the back slope on his hands and knees, painfully aware that others had left, pursued all the way by probing bullets fired, he supposed, by a Japanese marksman who did not have him in view. Some yards back, during a lull, he paused in a prone position to recover his breath and take stock of himself.

He knew that his own personal pack was somewhere off to the left and he had no intention of leaving without it. The search took perhaps two minutes. He had just checked it over and was about to sling it on his back when a weapon of heavier calibre took up the song of death.

Projectiles flew in an arc. Some hit the tree above him, loosening dusty parasitic moulds which fell around his shoulders. Thoroughly rattled, he dived sideways. He never saw the bared tree root which tripped him. His crown connected with an unyielding tree bole and his senses left him at once . . .

* * *

A put-put noise penetrated his consciousness first. Not an unpleasant sound. Mingled with it were other little bits of background noises. The bubbling of water, and then voices which were unintelligible like a record played far too quickly.

Before his eyes opened, he had a sensation of floating, as though he was dancing along without body weight and carrying something on his head. And then he knew he was feeling pain, and not carrying a weight. He came to slowly, blinking hard and his first reaction was that he had slept with his sun spectacles on.

He raised them unbelievingly and studied lush grass and fallen leaves close to his face. He was lying prone. Something about his situation seemed familiar, but he knew that there was a problem of sorts. His head throbbed. He closed his eyes and opened them again.

Some twenty yards away from him was the pool where the troops had swum. Recollection then came with a tantalising rush. The commandos had pulled out. Peyton had been killed, or at least severely wounded. He was alone: devoid of friends. But not altogether alone. There was a motor launch not far away with the engine running.

Sticking up above the rim of the inlet was a green object which appeared to have life. A green cloth object, round in shape with a flap to it. A jockey cap! The approved headgear of a Japanese soldier in jungle warfare.

Excited voices speaking in a foreign tongue. The Japs had come over. The jockey cap disappeared, but only momentarily. He knew that he was likely to be discovered at any moment. The water. He had to get down in the water before the search began. He moved a few inches, collected his knapsack and began to crawl, inch by inch, head first down the slope towards the lapping waters.

He had not been moving many seconds when about a dozen soldiers of Imperial Nippon swarmed up the slope at the rear of the inlet and took stock of the surrounding terrain. Orders were barked in a loud voice. Others took up the relaying of the orders and the men started to spread out and search.

Britwell increased his rate of progress, hidden from the questing eyes only by the bulk of a teak tree and a bunch of roots which protruded above the surface of the soil. He stiffened as the engine of the launch was opened up. Shortening his grip on the strap of his knapsack, he turned sideways and rolled several feet down the slope, fetching up with a slight jolt against the gnarled probing roots of a mangrove-type tree.

A tiny landslide followed him. Soil pattered round his face. One Japanese soldier was clearly visible to him, so that he could see the big hip pockets of the drab green trousers and the shine where the man had worn them thin through sitting down.

Hauling himself forward with the help of the roots, he did a slow seal dive into the water. His progress seemed maddeningly slow. He felt the wetting progress reach his waist, his hips and then his lower calves. At last he was under, with only bubbles and a few ripples to mark his entry.

Seconds later, he allowed the top of his head to show, fully expecting the business end of a rifle to be pointing in his direction, but he had been lucky. The Nippon infantrymen were fanning out to search the banks on both sides of the inlet. He breathed through his mouth, at the same time grabbing his hat, which had floated off. Next he removed his spectacles.

Under a slippery forbidding arch of roots he drew in and secured his knapsack and cautiously regulated his breathing. He had a queer feeling that he was in for a long wait. All manner of disquieting thoughts went through his head. He saw again Peyton's body being jerked about by machine gun bullets. His mind's eye showed him the rest of the troop being led expertly away from the *chaung* by Shan and his friends.

If he managed to avoid capture, he was still entirely on his own in an alien country, with no knowledge of local languages and no sort of training in bush warfare or in living off the land. Up to his neck in water, a sensation which for the present was pleasant, but which would become irksome as the day ebbed and the temperature dropped phenomenally low.

Someone cut the launch's engine, the first significant happening since he committed his body to water.

* * *

Britwell supposed that a European would find it hard to match Orientals for patience. He knew as he crouched under the mangrove roots that he was on an endurance test. At the outset, he did not know whether he could keep to the water long enough to ensure his freedom. A lot depended upon the Japanese, what they planned to do: whether they intended to stay.

His wrist watch continued to function well, even under water. Within the first hour, his bones began to creak. He had to stand after that with his head clear and take what support he could get for his back from the curving roots.

In the second hour, those Japanese who had not followed up the retreating British group began to relax. They bathed, listened to a radio and made a meal. Some time later, when his skin was becoming spongey due to continued soaking in water, they must have stretched out on the slope and taken a late siesta.

Towards eight o'clock, he decided to risk moving to another spot. Slowly and with absolute caution, he removed himself from the overhanging roots, floated on his back and gradually worked his way further from the inlet.

By eight-thirty, he was stretched out on his back with only his legs in the water. He was sure about the time because the launch's motor suddenly rattled into life and several excited shouts indicated that it was about to make a return run across the *chaung*. The lonely man felt a lifting of the spirits. It was as well he remained on the alert, however, because more delayed shouts revealed that not all the Jap personnel had boarded the boat.

Some were still on land, and that surely meant that they thought some of the British soldiers might still be in the area. More waiting. More anxiety, with the closer onset of night. Inevitably, the anxious loner dozed. He slept for almost two hours and did not know what it was that roused him to wakefulness.

The sky was clear and almost cloudless, but it had that certain quality about it which suggested that nightfall was imminent.

Britwell listened hard. His straining ears told him that a smouldering fire was still burning. Even after such a long delay, he knew he dared not take any chances. Two things stopped him from creeping away in the wake of his comrades. Firstly, he knew that a numerically superior Jap pursuit force would be between him and those he sought. Secondly, he had to find out all he could about the fate of young Ronnie Peyton before leaving the spot.

Something prompted him to stick to the water for a time. Checking that he had all his gear with him, he slipped back into the stream and patiently waded back along the way he had swum. There was no sign of any Jap party on the other side of the *chaung*. It was the near side which troubled him. He could see the faint glow of firelight up the rear slope beyond the inlet. However, there were no bodies reclining near it.

The light was fading appreciably by the minute. He pushed off and swam on a slow breaststroke past the inlet, heading inshore on the nearside of the land spit. The twisted body of his young friend was still there, apparently untouched since the Japs arrived. He felt certain that Peyton was dead, but he knew he had to get closer and make absolutely sure.

He was just about to rise up out of the water and go forward when a sudden warning hiss anchored him like a statue. The figure in white which ghosted towards him must have done the circuit of the pool. It was the youth, Shan, who threw himself down beside Britwell and held him back, entreating him not to emerge on the land spit.

'Please, sahib, you have exhibited great patience. Don't bring trouble to yourself by approaching your friend, as he is long since dead. There is danger by his body.'

At first, Britwell, who had recovered quite quickly from the shock of seeing another face, did not take in the last statement.

'But Shan, in a way I was responsible for him. Besides, I thought I saw a slight arm movement just now.'

The young Burmese bit his lip in anguish. 'It is possible that you saw a movement. The body will be booby-trapped. See, I have the camera. I went closer before I knew you were anywhere near.'

Britwell took the camera, examined it and studied the young guide in a new light. 'They left the body there expecting someone like me to go and touch it? I find that hard to believe.'

Shan shrugged. 'It is one of the ways in which the enemy make war. If you want, I could prove the body is rigged, but we would have to get out in a hurry.'

Fishing about beneath him in the shallow water, the Burmese produced a big smooth pebble. He tossed it up in his hand, as though preparing to throw it. At the same time, he studied Britwell's rather grim expression.

'You would have to be prepared to see your friend's body blown to pieces. Shall I toss this stone?'

Britwell thought: To take away my lingering doubts, have Ron Peyton's remains blown to bits?

He said: 'No, that won't be necessary. Naturally, I would have been more satisfied if I had the chance to give him a decent burial, but you know the local situation better than I. If you say it would be too dangerous, I'm prepared to leave without any further delay.'

'It is too dangerous, sahib,' Shan whispered, sighing with relief. 'I suppose your first aim is to rejoin your scattered party. Am I right?'

Britwell nodded. 'Certainly. I don't want to see this spot any more, although I suppose we could have lost many more personnel.'

'Let's go then,' the youth urged. 'Hanging about makes me nervous. Follow me round the pool and be alert in case I see the Jap rearguard.'

Britwell emerged thankfully from the water which had hidden him. His soaked boots squelched in the mud and his steps were uncertain. Shan took him well clear of the fire embers and slowed down when they were about a hundred yards into the trees.

Behind the same bulking tree bole, they rested and listened. Foreign muttering carried to them from the beginnings of the ill-marked path of retreat. Shan then grovelled around until he found another stone. He indicated by mime what he intended to do, and Britwell approved. In the gathering gloom, Shan had to be careful that his stone carried to his target. Had it fallen shorter, it was likely that the Japs would have stumbled across them.

Oddly enough, the missile did all that they intended it to do, and more. It pitched into the embers of the fire, scattering stones and half-consumed twigs before bouncing into the pool where it sent up quite a bit of spray.

The Jap's reaction was instantaneous. Suddenly a thicket spewed bodies. Urgent shouts were scarcely muffled as about four men darted off towards the water making little sound in their rubber-soled boots.

Britwell was about to speak in a normal tone of voice, but his companion clamped a hand over his mouth.

He whispered: 'Two or more soldiers stay behind. They hold the other end of the wire which made your friend's arm move.'

Britwell nodded and signified that he was ready to resume his escape through the gloom.

5

For upwards of a furlong, the two runaways were very careful about the sounds they made. Shan seemed to sense when the danger from the rear was over. He straightened his back and hummed a fetching Burmese song while Britwell stumbled along in his wake, marvelling at the nature of his good fortune.

No longer was he alone. No longer did he doubt the sincerity of his guide. About a mile and a half away from the *chaung*, the Burmese chopped his way through a bamboo thicket at an angle where his handiwork would not be too noticeable.

Some fifty yards off-track, he found a secluded grove. In a natural depression caused by the uprooting of a tree, he made a fire and signalled for Britwell to strip off his wet clothing. With the sudden sinking of the sun, the temperature had dropped quite low.

For a time, the journalist's teeth

chattered. By doing a few useful exercises and crouching by the fire, he managed to raise his body temperature. Shan slipped in and out of the clearing for a time, until he had sufficient fruit for them to eat. Britwell eked out their meal with some of his K rations. They had water but at that particular time neither of them felt excessively thirsty.

Under a wall shelter and partially covered by palm leaves, the ill-assorted couple sat down.

On his elbow, Britwell said his last words of the day. 'Shan, I have to thank you for coming back to me. Earlier in the day, the sergeant and I had doubts about you. Now, I'm certain that you are a friend of the British. If and when I can, I'll try to repay what you have done for me.'

Shan beamed with pleasure. In the flickering light of the fire his mobile features suggested that he was about to make certain revelations. He apparently thought better of them.

'I'm sorry your little outfit ran into trouble at the *chaung*. It was something I could not foresee.'

Britwell added words which put the youth at his ease. The silence closed in upon them. The green pigeons and parrots, disturbed by their approach, had settled down again. So had the apes and gibbons and the myriad insects which made the whole jungle seem to crawl at times.

The birds and animals would stay that way until dawn, or until the careless foot of intruding man disturbed them again. There was no need for anyone to stay awake.

★   ★   ★

Shan arose at dawn. He paused long enough for Britwell to make tea out of some partially dried leaves and shared more of his issued rations. Within a half hour, they were on their way. Soon, the youth spotted a track which led towards the north. Others had used it the previous day, but it was not easy to say whether it had been the British or the Japanese. Care was a necessity of movement throughout the forenoon.

At a fast walk, they made good progress, and towards noon Shan spotted the first of a series of tree 'blazes' left for him by his friends, the Boli brothers. In order to indicate the route they had taken, here and there they had hacked lumps out of the tree boles.

Lunch was a sketchy affair of palm shoots and a variety of different kind of fruit. Shan danced around while they were eating. All the time they rested, he was anxious to get on. At the same time, he was considerate about Britwell's performance. About the touch of athlete's foot which started between his toes.

'Sooner or later, sahib, you should try walking without your shoes. It will be good for your feet to toughen up. You will find it rather painful at first.'

'For the time being I will keep my boots on,' Scoop decided. 'As soon as you find some easy going I will try to perform barefoot.'

Shan giggled, and on they went again. The guide picked out many signs, some of them left deliberately and others which his knowledge of jungle lore told him about the others ahead of him. By early afternoon, he made it clear that in his opinion the Japs were not following up the British soldiers' trail.

As they paused and smoked a cigarette between them they talked about distances. 'I believe we shall overtake your friends in an hour. I think I know where Yusuf and Ahmed have taken them. If I am right, we have a choice. We can follow up right behind them, or I can make a detour which will put us ahead of them.'

'Make the detour, Shan, by all means. And what about the location we talked about? The grassland. You said it would take about a day's journey. How far are we from that?'

Shan seemed to find it hard to talk in actual figures. 'When your friends ran away from the *chaung*, they did not take the shortest route. It is possible my friends did not manage to persuade them straight away about the right way to go.

'But it should be possible to get close to the grassland during the dark hours of tonight, if your meeting time is soon.

77

Perhaps you will believe me now, sahib, when I say there are no British troops at the place you say. Moreover, it is dangerous, I think.'

Thumping his thigh with his fist, Britwell insisted. 'But it was part of our orders. Even if there are no British troops there now, Shan, they will come. We shall be aware of them.'

Shan shrugged, frowned, turned his thoughts to other matters of great moment to himself, and finally walked off again. After that, Britwell had the impression that he was moving in a curve. There were no more blazed marks on account of the detour.

After changing direction in a small glade between teak and bamboo which had the appearance upon arrival of a bird sanctuary, the youth headed directly across country. Thirty minutes was sufficient for him to get confirmation of his whereabouts.

'Presently, sahib, we come to a *chaung*. A different one this time. One which has had no water in it for many months. A dry one. I believe your friends are moving up the *chaung* bed and that we are ahead of them. If we are, you will be able to exercise your bare feet in the sand.'

Britwell grinned. ' 'Barefoot in Burma.' How would that be for a newspaper article title?'

'A newspaper article?' the youth repeated. He was puzzled.

'The young photographer who died worked on the same newspaper as I do. We came into this war zone to take photographs and to write about the war and the people, as we find them. I am very sad about my young friend. It was because of me that he came.'

'I have noticed that you carry no gun. Did you have to come to Burma?'

Britwell frowned, and rested a hand on the youth's shoulder. 'I didn't have any choice. I insisted on being sent abroad and I had to come here. The jungle war is very different from war in Europe.'

'I'm glad you came, sahib, and I hope you get back safely.'

'Thank you, Shan. You have no idea how glad I am I met you on my first assignment in your country.'

Five minutes later, they slipped down the bank of the *chaung* and settled down to rest. The youth spent a lot of time studying the sandy bottom for signs of footprints. At the same time, Britwell removed his shoes and tinkered with the camera.

Shan's sensitive ears picked up new sounds about twenty minutes later. He made their presence known to his friends by imitating the sounds made by one of the local parrots. The Boli brothers came ahead of the others and embraced the youth. McCool and his men came more cautiously, halting as soon as they saw figures ahead of them.

Britwell took a photograph of them and presently the two groups fused, relief showing on all their faces.

* * *

Eight hours later, McCool's unit was safely hidden in a belt of scrub less than half a mile south of the cleft between two ridges. Several miles had been covered since mid-afternoon when Britwell and

Shan rejoined the rest.

Shan and his countrymen had appeared to be more and more perplexed as they journeyed further north and then to westward. They appeared to be gripped by pessimism and disapproved of the soldiers' insistence upon visiting the scene of a remote grassland against advice. While the Europeans settled back and eased their packs, the Burmese gathered in a tight trio and murmured among themselves.

McCool, who had less confidence in the natives than Britwell, studied them from a few yards away as dusk fell.

Corporal Judd chuckled. 'There she goes, Scoop, instant darkness! Just as if me mother had switched the lights out. Coo, them native boys' natural camouflage don't 'alf work well in the dark, don't it?'

The sergeant grunted. 'Tell me, Britwell, straight up! What do you make of all this?'

'I think number one airstrip site is just through those ridges. I'm coming round to the view that no one landed a couple of nights ago. No one only us, that is.'

'What makes you think that then?'

McCool persisted.

'Nothing special,' Britwell tried to explain. 'Just a feeling I have. If the rest of your outfit had landed according to plan, we'd have seen signs of them before this.'

'Oh, I don't know,' Judd argued. 'Not if they were deliberately keepin' out of sight till the parachutists arrive.'

'You could be right,' the journalist conceded, 'but I still have a feeling that our Burmese guides would have known something about it.' He turned over and blinked as Shan crawled up to his shoulder. 'What is it, Shan?'

'Sahib, we think there is danger here. To the east, sunrise way, there are many Japanese. Also a road and a railway. Much traffic. A river, too.'

'But that doesn't explain about here, Shan, where we were supposed to go! What about here? Can't you tell us anything?'

'I regret that the information we have is not up to date. This place is a long way from our village. All we can say is that we think the enemy may be closer than you think!'

Britwell patted Shan's shoulder and gestured for him to wait. The youth tried a mild protest, but no one took any notice of him because a few seconds earlier the keenest ears in the unit had heard the distant throb of aircraft engines.

The sound alerted and unified the party like nothing else could. It came from the north-west, the general direction of Imphal and India. Was it Japanese or British? No one really thought the forces of Imperial Nippon would operate their aircraft this far north in Burma, but the idea had to be considered.

Britwell murmured: 'Jap bombers or British paratroops?'

'I could swear those are ours,' Everton remarked firmly.

Shan clicked his tongue. 'The Japs only use planes of that sort for bombing, but what would they bomb here? There is nothing of sufficient importance from a military point of view. The planes are British. I think the British and the Japanese are both here.'

The youth's last warning was overlooked. McCool wriggled across to him.

'If it's our air force, they'll be droppin' both men and supplies! We ought to get closer in order to help. Never mind about the risks. You understand?'

With the neck of his smock twisted in the fist of the sergeant Shan had to understand. There was a short consultation between the Boli brothers and their leader. The unit stood to, and a few seconds later they were heading for the gap as though it was Shangri-la.

*　*　*

At the same time exactly, the greater part of the grassland beyond the two ridges ruffled its surface. It stretched in a north-south direction; for many seasons the grasses which had grown upon it had been of the short variety which only extended to a few inches.

In the past few days it had acquired tree boles, trunks with a difference. These had been sawn down in another area, transported to the 'field', and laid out flat, across-wise, thus causing insurmountable difficulties for any aircraft which chose to squeeze down on the grass for the first time.

The ruffling of the surface occurred when the reclining Japanese infantrymen who were stretched out flat adjacent to the four-score or more felled tree trunks shifted their positions for the last time before action. They wriggled in closer to the teak boles and pulled their leafy camouflage over them.

In the trees to the east, a large silent unit of anti-aircraft and searchlight troops checked over their equipment for the last time.

The officer-in-charge, a very tall hollow-cheeked individual with bowed legs, was stalking from one group to another gripping his sword, still sheathed, in his right hand. On other occasions he had it drawn, but this was one time when he did not want to give the alarm by reflecting light from the steel of the blade.

He spoke to his junior officers and NCOs in whispers, counselling patience and caution. His own continuous stalking showed that his problem was as troublesome as theirs.

Meanwhile, the British paratroop carriers altered course to the north of the strip and the first aircraft flew down its length at a modest height. The tension mounted in the planes, alongside of the grassland, and a little further south where the glider men were working their way through a gap and seeking a commanding position on the inner slope, west side.

When it was seen that the plane was going to overshoot without disgorging its human contents, the strain was almost too much for some of those waiting on the ground. A youthful Japanese lieutenant, for instance, almost ruined the ambush by putting his searchlights into action prematurely.

Only just in time, the senior officer got along to him and countermanded the order to switch on. The pilot of the leading craft banked and swung away to starboard, having decided rather late on that he was not giving his jumpers sufficient altitude for a safe drop.

Back he went to the north, where he turned again and assumed the lead over the others, who were circling. This time he was well over six hundred feet as he flew south. He flashed the green light in the rear section of his fuselage, and the standing men, with their statichute cords attached to a bar above their heads, bunched up and prepared to go earthwards.

The leader tumbled clear, spinning awkwardly for a few seconds in the buffeting slipstream. And then his parachute opened. It opened and spun behind him and finally granted him an upright pose. Others followed in rapid succession.

The blossoming mushrooms of silk with their smocked owners dangling beneath them had a remarkable effect upon the youthful Japanese searchlight officer. He who had almost 'blown' the ambush before felt compelled to use his lights on the first half dozen parachutists to sail to earth. The arena was instantly floodlit.

As a direct consequence of his action, the men hidden upon the ground revealed themselves prematurely and started firing hopefully at the nearest target. Most of the paratroops died quickly. A few of their number, those discharged last from the same plane, swung away to westward of the strip. Unknown to them, the west side was the one least populated with the enemy.

In spite of the sluggishness of his aircraft, the pilot of the lead plane took immediate evasive action. He was later to get his crate back to base, even though the fuselage was breached in places. The other planes reacted even quicker, banking away sharply before the anti-aircraft guns could line up on them.

The searchlight operators concentrated upon the falling figures until they ran out of victims. Consequently, the planes were well scattered and difficult to trace by the time the senior officer had beheaded the blunderer and relayed fresh orders by loud hailer.

6

When the lights first flashed on the Lancastrians were still toiling up the north slope of the west side of the gap between the two ridges. Shan, McCool and Britwell were at the front with the others strung out behind them and making good progress.

As the first blinding arc split the gloom over the grassland the leading trio came to a sudden halt, transfixed by a glimmering of the appalling nature of the ambush. The commandos stumbled into them, their startled eyes looking elsewhere.

Britwell gripped McCool's upper arm as they stared open-mouthed at the dangling smock-clad figures sailing to earth. 'Our guides couldn't have been more correct when they warned us, sarge.'

'I know, I know, mate, but it was a chance we had to take. Trouble is, what do we do now?'

'Go to earth for a few minutes till you work out a plan of action. I have a feeling any sort of diversion on our part would be ill-timed.'

A single terse order was enough to send every man down into cover. With startling rapidity the grim pageant developed, shocking the seasoned watchers who had experienced tough clashes in Italy, the North African desert and elsewhere.

Britwell's thoughts were chaotic. He noted that the whole area was strewn with tree boles and that for every tree there was a Jap infantryman simply lying back and blasting off with a light automatic weapon as the parachutes floated down.

One or two of the sky troopers managed to get in a counter burst from their Sten guns but it was likely that they did not eliminate more than half a dozen of the formidable enemy force.

A murmuring spread through the watchers. The Burmese withdrew a few yards and talked among themselves. Britwell gnawed a knuckle and ruefully totted up what the commandos had achieved since their premature drop from the skies. Nothing! And at this juncture, it looked as if they had no future.

In desperation, of course, they could pit their fighting power against the superior enemy, but it would end inevitably in their total annihilation.

Everton, whose shoulder had ceased to give him trouble, murmured: 'I say, sarge. Bloody hell! We've *got* to do something. We can't just sit here an' watch our boys bein' shot to ribbons!'

'The other planes are pulling out! That's one good thing,' Britwell commented. 'It looks bad now, but it could have been a bigger disaster. The Japs are slow to use their ack-ack guns.'

'Don't anybody shoot unless I say so,' McCool ordered, in a tense voice.

'It'll be over in a minute or two,' Britwell murmured in his ear.

The sergeant glared at him, his teeth clenched. He felt he was a fighting man in a position he should never have been placed. Where he could not hit out without precipitating trouble which would lead to the deaths of his comrades.

Suddenly the searchlights switched

from the arena to the planes which were taking evasive action. The ground vibrated with the recoil of the high angle weapons. McCool rose slowly to his feet, struggling towards a decision. With heavier calibre weapons they could have shot out some of the lights, but at a grave cost in losses.

Britwell commented: 'Two or three 'chutes floated into those trees to westward. It might be possible to rescue them, if you're determined to do something positive. I just hope we don't get widely scattered as a result.'

McCool filled his chest to make an announcement, and then let out the air again.

'Look here, you men. I haven't enjoyed watchin' this slaughter any more than you 'ave. In fact, it means all our efforts since we landed have come to naught. I'm goin' to take a few blokes into those trees to try an' rescue the parachutists. But most of you will have to stay here an' keep quiet, because we'll have to come out again in this direction.'

McCool forcibly rejected Mick Judd by pushing him in the chest. Two tall dark brothers from Bootle received similar treatment. While Britwell was ascertaining whether Shan would go with them, the sergeant picked out Everton and Willie More and decided that with Britwell and the boy guide that would be enough.

The grumbling was short-lived.

'What do I do if I don't make it back, sarge?' Judd asked humbly.

McCool coughed and spat out. 'Lean on the guides. We need a friendly billet. Then get in touch with base by radio. Use any opportunity to hit back, but don't get too involved.'

Having delivered himself of the advice, the senior NCO then realized the implications behind it. He drew in breath sharply, gestured farewell to his old comrades and finally hurried away, drawing Shan with him.

The constant echo of insects on the move was back again, due to the artificial light and human activity. Reduced to five, and treading almost on one another's heels, the would-be rescuers moved away to westward, gradually working their way lower. The planes had made off, the searchlights had been cut out altogether and the only light visible came from a few lamps amid the trees where the anti-aircraft squad was located.

Ten minutes was sufficient time to reach the level of the grassland. At the lower level, there was always the chance of meeting prowling Japs also looking for survivors. The tension grew among the tiny group.

No one asked Shan what he thought, and he merely did his duty as a guide, seeking out the fugitives and alert for sounds made by the enemy. He led them successfully around the edge of the arena and entered the trees without running into any other humans.

Five minutes of probing into virgin teak saw them fifty yards in from the perimeter but lacking success in their search. Their nerves were jumping long before the sinister rattle of the machine-gun, off to their right. All five jumped to face the sound. In a heap they crouched near the earth and wondered at the outcome.

'That was one of theirs,' Britwell murmured.

'Yer, that was a woodpecker, all right,' McCool agreed, 'but what did it mean? One of our boys likely copped it, an' we've got company here in the woods. Lead us forward, lad.'

Shan started to protest that any rush to the same spot might get them all eliminated, but McCool brushed aside the risk, conceding only a minute's rest before going on. They started to be aware of the flapping parachute almost at once. It required a great effort of will to avert the eyes from it in search of the elusive machine-gunner and his party.

The paratrooper was still under it, swinging gently in a grotesque turning movement caused by a light breeze. His head was lolling and his left side was out of shape. He was dead. Nothing was to be gained by staying near to him.

Shan peered into McCool's face, wondering if he had searched enough. The determined expression and the pointing finger started them all off again, still heading northwards. A half mile of cautious going did them little good. Faint lights showing across the open eventually made the sergeant accede to Shan's request for a change of direction.

Next, they turned west. Three to four hundred yards in that direction led to no further discoveries. After that, they turned south again, conscious of the slow passing of time and wondering how their mates were making out on the side of the ridge.

Everton, who was using his excellent night vision on the upper parts of the trees rather than the earth, broke the tension they were all feeling by stumbling over a body. To everyone's surprise, it was a Japanese. That meant one or two survivors were on the ground and still active. So thought the British, but Shan was not so sure. His groping hands told him that the Jap soldier had died by a broad-bladed knife which had been thrown or thrust into the chest.

Half an hour later, they came upon a second parachute, one which was empty. Great caution was used in searching the immediate area closely, but there was no sign of the soldier who had been released from it and moved on.

Britwell sensed a sudden uplifting in the party's spirits. He marvelled that the possibility of one survivor could so boost them, and wondered what the outcome of the whole exercise would be. While he was still pondering, McCool called for a change of plan.

'Now look here, lads. That fellow we're lookin' for had a long way to drop. He might have damaged an ankle or busted a knee. So we have to spread out an' search, in case he's crippled. Understand? This time we fan out in a straight line an' work our way south. Any sort of alarm, a bit of finger snappin' will 'elp. That all right by you, young Shan?'

'Er, yes, I suppose so, sergeant. I was thinking about something else.'

The NCO gave the guide a hard look which the darkness partially dispelled. And then they were moving again, with Shan and the sergeant in the middle, Britwell on the left flank and the two soldiers on the right.

An hour of slow prowling with the nerves on edge for every sound, and no result. No one believed that the survivor could have moved far from his landing spot. There was a brief argument, at the end of which McCool asserted his authority. Shan's notion that the missing man might have been spirited away by friends was discounted, and the five settled down to rest in a small circle with each of them looking outwards.

Weariness and the compelling blackness soon sapped their will to stay awake. First one and then another drifted off into sleep. At times three out of the five were sleeping soundly. Dawn was less than an hour away when the leader sought to assert himself again.

He shook everybody. 'It's about time we were movin',' he announced. 'If we're to get through that gap with the rest of our boys before daylight. Our efforts have not amounted to much, but at least we can say we've tried. So let's get back up that slope. Everybody ready?'

No one wanted extra time. Everyone was upstanding and willing: off they went with Dick McCool maintaining a strong pace alongside of young Shan, who seemed to be tireless.

* ★ ★

Twenty minutes later they were silently apprehended on the side of the ridge by Mick Judd who had been awake all night, and the Blade brothers who hailed from Bootle. The bleak-eyed trio reluctantly put up their weapons. Everton and More rushed forward to join their mates, leaving Judd to confer with McCool and Britwell.

'I see you've still got your full number, sarge, without any extras, but what kept you? Before you answer that, I have to report that our two guides vamoosed shortly after you went off. I don't suppose you've seen anything of them? Any chance Shan is likely to pull out, as well?'

Shan, who was some distance away, managed to overhear what was said about the Boli brothers. He did not seem surprised.

After concluding a brief explanation, McCool moved in upon Shan who was ringed by several of the others.

'Now look here, Shan,' the sergeant began, 'I can't rightly hold you responsible for the antics of your friends, but you don't seem surprised they ran off. Now, I want us to clear off this ridge as soon as possible. I don't need to tell you why. You wanted us to go to your village when we first met. Well now you're goin' to get the chance to take us.'

'I think you should wait just a few minutes, sergeant. I have a very good reason for saying so. Please wait.'

McCool snorted, backed off and appeared to be brewing up for a fierce show of temper. He was forestalled, however, when the youngster snapped his fingers and pointed back in the same direction as the searchers had come from. Presently, he trotted off. When Britwell, who had followed, overtook him, he was assisting the brothers Boli to bring in a paratrooper with a broken leg.

The journalist took a corner of the stretcher improvised out of bamboos and lianas reinforced by leaves. On it was a thickset auburn-haired fellow in his middle thirties with his left leg bandaged to bamboo splints.

'Good morning, chaps. My word, you

are well organized out here. Good of you to send your orderlies out looking for me. Don't know what I'd have done without them, seeing as how I broke a bone on landing.'

'Keep your voice down, if you don't mind, brother,' Britwell advised. 'I'm glad they found you. Some of us have been out all night looking for you. The unit is on the point of moving out. How did they fix your leg?'

A minute later, the rescued man was set down in the middle of the tired Commandos who studied him with eyes narrowed. Clearly, Judd wanted to have words with the Bolis, but they did not give him an opportunity.

'Not bad, not bad at all,' the survivor admitted. 'If you could just spare a couple of minutes before we pull out I'd be obliged, though. I don't think the splints are doing a proper job. The whole thing aches, don't you know.'

'I'll take a look at it,' Britwell promised.

Within a very short space of time the latter discovered that the break across the shin had not been put together properly.

As the makeshift first aid had been done in darkness, there was no cause for grievance.

'I believe I can improve it for you,' Scoop enthused. 'Maybe I ought to give you a couple of pills to kill the pain first.'

The patient shrugged, but agreed. Britwell broke out the medical kit and studied a row of glass tubes holding pills. He selected one and turned aside to open it cautiously. There was a quick movement beside him and an even quicker withdrawal.

The patient started to chuckle, but Corporal Judd's voice was far above a whisper as he complained. 'Did you see that, sarge?'

'See what?' McCool asked, without interest. He was having a couple of drags on a fag end cupped in the palm of his hand.

'Shan dipped his hand in the medicines, here. He whipped up a tube and went off so fast I can't see him any more.'

McCool swore. He drove his butt end into the ground and turned to face the stretcher and those grouped around it.

'Send somebody after him, you fool. Two men. Jack an' Sam Blade. Tell them not to go far, though. It's vital we clear out in the next ten minutes.'

Others went after the Blade brothers long before ten minutes were up. As was expected, Shan had vanished. The Bolis looked embarrassed, but offered no sort of explanation. Britwell, who was just finishing his chores as medical orderly, wondered if the Burmese youngster had known what he was taking.

In fact, the missing tube contained quinine, used in the treatment of fevers and possibly other tropical ailments.

7

The men of the small detachment were tired, frustrated and angered by the events of the night and the sudden withdrawal of the youth, Shan. None more so than Sergeant McCool, upon whom the weight of responsibility was beginning to tell. However, he needed no prompting to carry out his intended withdrawal before the unwelcome arrival of dawn left them a prey to the many hostiles in the district.

While the commandos were fidgetting about and checking their gear, the NCO drew aside the Boli brothers, and spoke sharply to them. 'You two are goin' to earn your keep today. So as to get clear of the Japs we have to withdraw through the gap. After that, you will lead us to your village, an' no runnin' off on your own like your chum did! Savvy?'

The Burmese brothers seemed pleased and anxious to move off. In daylight, they were distinguishable because one of them wore gold earrings, while the other had a short knife scar down his left cheek.

'Yes, yes, sahib, we understand and like your instructions. But we must go quickly. We will act as scouts in the first mile. It is best that way.' Ahmed, the more vocal of the two, spoke for both.

'No,' McCool argued, 'you will carry the stretcher.'

This time the natives looked distressed. 'Sahib, you have made a bad decision,' Ahmed remarked, tugging nervously at one of his earrings.

Ahmed then stepped to the fore end of the stretcher, but indicated for his brother, Yusuf, to get to the head of the column. The latter hurried forward without hesitation, in spite of the blatant anger showing in the NCO's face.

'Any other time I'd have your bloody ears off, mates,' he muttered fiercely.

Ginger More moved nearer to him and murmured in sympathy. 'Sooner or later, you're goin' to have a showdown with that surly pair, sarge.'

'Don't I know it,' the sergeant retorted.

'Now, you, Ginger, get hold of the back end of that stretcher an' mind you don't stumble with it.'

The redhead, taken aback, wondered where to put his weapon. He was carrying a Sten gun at the time. Britwell relieved him of it and at once they moved off. Already the sky in the east was turning from black to dark grey. Dawn was imminent. There was a distant sound, as of thunder heralding its approach.

The descent was a cautious, risky, uncertain business. Yusuf was some ten yards ahead of McCool, who had difficulty in keeping up with him. Two commandos followed, the Blade brothers, and then the stretcher. The rest of the squad brought up the rear. The man being carried was strangely silent. Perhaps he knew the odds against them as well as his bearers.

Britwell, for once, broke the strict rule of the snake column by walking along a line about five yards below the others. The Sten, although a lightweight weapon of its kind, weighed heavily on his right arm. He hoped he would not be called upon to use it because he did not expect to be anything like proficient without training and, in any case, he was not supposed to fire on the enemy as a non-combatant.

The lightening greyness of the dawn sky was suddenly ripped asunder by thin veins of light, and still there were no special signs of activity from the thickets populated by the Japanese. Men who had recently been shivering due to the appallingly low night temperatures now began to stream with perspiration. The sun was still not with them, but the tension and the anxiety involved in withdrawing within striking distance of a vastly superior enemy force told on them.

Every now and then, a man slipped, but no one made any sort of a clatter and no serious harm was done. Those at the rear of the column had confidence as they followed in the footsteps of their mates. Britwell, off to one side, began to see why the snake column routine was such a good one.

He encountered roots and boulders which the others missed. There were diabolically prickly bushes to be avoided and always the chance of leeches, red ants and the occasional snake. He gave even more of his concentration to the going underfoot. So engrossed was he that his lack of interest in their surroundings might have caused a disaster.

His boot toe had recently caught in an eroded root and this had caused him to lose ground. A sudden feeling that all was not well made him look up. At first he saw nothing, and then the perspiration spurted from his forehead as he saw a single Jap with a rifle rise up further down the slope and draw a bead on someone in the line.

Britwell eased to a stop, licked his lips and started to bring up the Sten. He was moving it slowly so as not to give away his own position to the Jap when something flew through the air. A sound which came out like a polite cough was emitted by the Japanese as the broad point of a thrown *dah* entered his chest and penetrated his heart.

The unfortunate man sank to the ground with very little sound. Britwell met over his body with Yusuf, who had come to collect his knife. The Burmese' somewhat homely features relaxed into a broad smile, showing formidable white teeth. Pressing a foot on the victim's chest, Yusuf withdrew his weapon, wiping the blade rather carefully on the Jap's tunic. Britwell offered him the Japanese rifle, but he refused it, his attention roving over the nearest terrain to make sure the dead man had been alone.

The rest had kept going. The incident had proved to Britwell that there were others more capable than he for work on the flank. He hurried after the others until he came up with the stretcher. More gave him a strange look as he placed the Sten and the acquired rifle into the hands of the wounded man. Ginger's puzzlement was even greater as the journalist insisted upon taking over Ahmed's position at the front.

'Off you go, Ahmed, your brother needs your support as a scout and guard. He had just disposed of a Jap who had you in his sights. Take the rifle, just in case.'

Ahmed accepted this change of plan

with a good grace. He took the rifle, gave up his position and half-bowed to Britwell as he slipped away and commenced his vigil on the lower flank. As he did so, the first bright rays of the sun began to slant into the arena with its felled trees and grotesque corpses.

★   ★   ★

Within ten minutes the party was in the gap and treading warily towards the south. The sky was brightening all about them. Visibility dispersed the terrors of the night and substituted for them a new set of nerve janglers connected with the enemy and the knowledge that they were alone in unfamiliar country and unlikely to be reinforced in the near future.

Gradually the gap between their own little column and the superior Jap force on the grassland side widened. Britwell, although fit, was unaccustomed to working as a porter. His arms and back began to ache and only an indomitable desire not to let himself down in front of the professional soldiers kept him plugging away at his self-appointed chore for as long as he did.

The pace slackened as the heat penetrated to lower levels. Presently, bodily discomfort began to affect the wounded man. In order to distract himself from his own ordeal, Britwell began to converse with the paratrooper.

'You feel fit enough to talk back there?'

'Why, sure, old man. What do you want to talk about? Anything in particular?'

'Your name, rank and number would do for a start,' Britwell murmured, with a wry grin.

The wounded man chuckled. 'Jeremy Vallance, actually. First lieutenant, fifth Parachute Squadron, Home Counties Light Infantry. At your service. One time steeplechase jockey, sportsman in general. No fixed occupation in peacetime. I say, those flashes you're wearing. Oughtn't I to know you?'

'Harry Britwell, on the staff of the *Globe* newspaper. Getting into difficulties, as usual. I suppose that you are the senior officer present, if you have a couple of pips.'

'Nice to know you, Britwell. I don't know so much about taking charge of this outfit, though, especially with a broken leg. I guess it will be as well to leave Sergeant McCool in full control, in case he decides I'm too much of a burden and dumps me.'

Ginger More glowered at the pair of them. The look on his face suggested that he would not give a handful of coppers for the pair of them as fighting men. The only time the young Liverpudlian showed any proper interest in the conversation was when Britwell asked Vallance if he had any special knowledge of wireless-telegraphy and received a negative answer.

* * *

Half an hour later, Britwell sent word forward for McCool to appoint reliefs as stretcher bearers. In order to be avenged on the journalist the sergeant delayed ten minutes before putting the Blade brothers in as substitutes. Nevertheless, as soon as he was relieved, Scoop put all other considerations aside and went after the NCO.

At first, McCool was as cool as his name suggested, and aggressive.

'Britwell, if I tell one of these coolie lads to do a carryin' chore, there's no reason for you to intervene. Even if they would have been better employed as scouts. Now, what do you want?'

'What are your plans for getting in touch with your base?'

'If you are thinking about radio, I don't have an operator. Even if that spare set works. The operator was in our sister glider, the one piloted by my oppo, Lofty.'

'I know the wave-length they operate on. Wouldn't it be as well to ask for instructions?'

'You mean straightforward talking over the air? No code nor nothing to disguise what we're sayin'?'

'If we've got no operator what alternative do we have? If the Japs pick up the message we could get chased around a bit, but surely that's part of the business, isn't it? To keep superior enemy forces running around the countryside?'

McCool started to shake his head and rasp a thumb nail along his chin stubble, but his mind was not altogether closed to the new suggestion.

⋆   ⋆   ⋆

At noon precisely, Britwell donned the ear-phones and knelt beside the radio receiver. McCool and Judd crouched anxiously on the other side of it, while the rest of the outfit had spread themselves around a narrow glade in a position some few miles south-east of the airstrip which was not to be.

The journalist licked his lips, reflected upon his own gradual and inevitable involvement with the commandos and clicked a switch.

'Hello, this is *Migrant*. *Migrant* calling nature reserve Lalaghat. New Migratory regions unsuitable. Request instructions at thirteen hundred hours. Over and out.'

Just that. Britwell wondered if it would do the trick, and whether the sky troops base commanders on the Assam border would think their plight important enough to come through with specific instructions for the future.

Only the regular denizens of the jungle gave notice of their presence as the intruders attempted to get what rest was possible in that imaginatively protracted sixty minutes. Only the Bolis seemed to be at peace with themselves.

Promptly on the hour, the message came through. First, a few bars of an old traditional English melody, which made most of the tensed-up soldiers believe that their lean civvy had mucked things up by getting the wrong wavelength. And then the voice. A cultured one, but rather high-pitched.

'Sanctuary calling *migrant*. Sanctuary calling *migrant*. Proceed to hill market village, east river and contact the huntsman. Go to hill market village and contact the huntsman.'

No signing off by the voice. Just the old English melody repeated and then a sudden cut-out. Judd prompted Britwell to take off the ear-phones and also switch off the set. Others crowded round the puzzled newspaperman. The Bolis bobbed up at the rear of the group.

'Well?' McCool demanded to know, almost defiantly.

'What was all that bloody music?' More muttered.

Britwell blinked, lifted his sun spectacles and rubbed his eyes, before telling them what they wanted to know. 'We are to go to a hill market village on the east side of the river, and contact the huntsman. Does that make sense to any of you?'

One or two soldiers had abortive flashes of inspiration, but none of the suggestions took them anywhere, other than that the route was east again, and the location across a river. As the group started to break up, Ahmed Boli snapped his fingers.

'Please sahib, our village is the hill market village. There is no mystery in the message. To us it is most clear.'

This utterance braced most of the frustrated party, but McCool took a lot of convincing, as usual. 'There must be lots of hill market villages in this God-forsaken country. What makes you think yours is the one?'

Patiently, Ahmed explained. 'We come

from Daung Bazar, which translated means 'the market of the hill village.' That is where we are going.'

He could have added that Shan wanted them to go to the village from the outset, and that much time had been lost, but the time was not ripe for such a complaint.

'You know the huntsman, Ahmed?' Britwell queried.

'Yes, yes, we know him,' Yusuf blurted out. 'There is something to do with an English piece of music.'

'I believe the huntsman uses the code-name of John Peel,' Britwell added. 'That was the music they were playing.'

No one thought to doubt the journalist's conclusions, but More, who was in a disgruntled state of mind, spat into the grass and remarked that the huntsman was probably a very fat village headman with too many wives for his own good.

* * *

The journey eastwards continued without abatement throughout most of the afternoon. Lieutenant Vallance dozed fitfully as successive pairs of commandos carried him along.

On one occasion, Japanese planes flew low over them in sparse jungle. Later, as they negotiated another maze of paths on the way to the river, Yusuf pointed up into the trees which dwarfed them. Swinging very gently was a dead Japanese sniper, hanging like a stringless marionette by a broad leather belt which had been holding him to the tree. His machine-gun was still up there, probably unfired. The handle of a knife protruded from his chest. It had been thrown from below.

The sight of the sniper was disturbing and at the same time revealing. It gave further evidence of widespread Jap activity and hinted at other units opposed to the forces of Imperial Nippon apart from themselves.

Britwell noted these things in his writer's mind, but for quite a long time as they tramped east he was wondering about Shan, and whether he would have gone straight back to Daung Bazar with the quinine tablets or to some other location.

8

Towards five o'clock in the afternoon, Harry Britwell began to feel out of sorts with himself. At first he thought he might have picked up some sort of infection, but when his thoughts started to race he recognized signs of his old malady, the need to write down his thoughts on paper.

No one was more pleased when the Bolis suggested a short halt for rest and refreshment in a hollow some fifty yards off the track they were following. Britwell joined in with the chores and listened to the moans and gossip for a few minutes.

McCool voiced some of the doubts of his men when he tried to pin down their guides to the distance between themselves and the river. The suggestion was that they were either being diverted, or that the river was further off than they had been led to believe.

Ahmed, the talkative Burmese, patiently explained that some of the shorter tracks which they could have taken showed signs of having been used recently. In order to minimise the risk of meeting the enemy they had deliberately diverted the party onto other paths.

With a pot of hot coffee in his hand, Britwell sat down with his back to a tree and began to write.

This small party of the South Lanca-shire Commandos has certainly had to adapt itself to some trying situations. There have been times when I thought some of them would have cut my throat for two pence, but now their attitude has become a little more healthy.

Since the broadcast instructions, they have put more trust in the guides and I am reluctantly accepted, even though some of them still look upon me as an outsider and a liability. As a unit, they are clannish. It surprises me that Judd, who doesn't come from their side of the Mersey, gets along with them so well.

I still don't know them very well, but I suspect that in a straightforward clash against similar numbers of the enemy they would give an excellent account of themselves. In the future, I think McCool will gradually learn to make use of the expert knowledge of the natives and that can only be for the best.

Now that we have an objective, the shocks of the bad landing and the setbacks to their parachute comrades at the grassland area are sinking into perspective.

Burma is a land apart. We are permanently in an atmosphere of papaya and banana trees, betel-nut palms and a variety of the same tree which grows unique white flowers. At times, we have heard the barking of deer. As we enter a new belt of trees green pigeons are disturbed and multi-coloured squawking parrots protest at our arrival into their midst.

The slightest breeze can cause a panic among strangers such as us. Huge thickets of bamboo make rustling noises. Swaying palm leaves have a noise all their own. The occasional fall of a coconut has sometimes made us dive for the earth.

What a pity that all the dazzling beauty of this vast land has to be disregarded in *case an elusive enemy catches us unawares. At night the cloying sweet scent of jasmine titillates the nostrils of friend and foe alike.*

By the time these words had been hastily committed to paper, there were signs of growing restlessness. Two or three troopers who had been teasing the parachutist about his posh accent, started to clamber to their feet and move off. Britwell was aware of a low chuckle some five yards behind him. He turned and saw that Ginger More was regarding him speculatively with a cigarette tilted high in the corner of his mouth.

''Ope you 'aven't put down any military information that could fall into enemy 'ands, mate,' he remarked.

Britwell stood up. 'Nothing like that, scouse. And you won't be getting any mentions in despatches, either. Not yet, anyway.'

There was something in More's attitude which niggled the journalist. Something difficult to pin down. On that particular occasion, there was a change in him but it was difficult to analyse. Britwell promised himself a closer study of the redheaded soldier when the opportunity presented itself.

★ ★ ★

Immediately following the break, McCool changed his routine a little. Instead of staying near the front of the column, he sent forward his 'townie', Willie More, who was supported by the Bolis. This latter pair seemed to stand up to the strain of the day's toil better than any of the white men. Moreover, they were used to divining one another's thoughts and imminent actions.

The sergeant insisted upon taking a spell of carrying the stretcher at this stage, his partner at the rear end being Everton, fully recovered from his early mishap. Britwell assumed a position some twenty yards behind the stretcher, with the brothers Blade bringing up the rear.

For upwards of an hour, the party moved steadily eastward without incident. From front to rear, they were spread over about seventy yards. Primary jungle, mostly teak and bamboo, hemmed them in close on either hand. All personnel except the scouts and the wounded man found themselves studying the apparent impenetrable stretches on either side, looking for sidetracks to break the gloom of the monotonously solid 'walls'.

The jungle of this type could be said to be neutral. It protected track travellers from anyone seeking them who happened to be a mere twenty or thirty yards off-track, but if a column had the misfortune to encounter an enemy party head on, in the same track, then it was likely to be extremely difficult to break out at the sides with sufficient speed to avoid a clash.

All this was known to the slowest thinkers of the commando outfit and therefore the matter of vigilance never had to be emphasised.

Occasionally, the bird noises put up when the leaders disturbed the local feathered population appeared to grow in volume. No one at the rear, however, paid any particular attention to such matters until the time when Ahmed and Yusuf together made their way back to the stretcher and lined up on either side of the bearers.

'Yer, what's botherin' you two locals *this* time?' McCool queried. He was breathing heavily owing to the weight of the parachutist.

'Please, sahib, we think you should be at the front,' Ahmed explained carefully, tugging at his right earring.

McCool sniffed, and Britwell moved a little closer, the better to overhear the exchanges. 'I'm inclined to agree with you, Johnnie, lad, but I'm doin' this stint on the stretcher to please my boys an' I planned to be a bearer for a while longer. So what's botherin' you?

'It can't be much, otherwise you wouldn't have abandoned your station, would you?'

Yusuf frowned, not immediately comprehending, but his brother explained in their own tongue and the scarred man's brow cleared.

'It's your man, sahib, the one with the bright hair.'

McCool's brows shot up. 'Ginger?

What's he done?' He glared, first at one of them and then at the other, as though daring them to say a wrong word about a man from his own street who had gone to school with his younger brother.

'He is making mocking noises at the birds,' Ahmed persisted.

Everton, at the rear end of the stretcher, had a sudden quiet fit of the giggles. He was a muscular energetic man in his late twenties with slightly rounded shoulders which made his height, five-feet eight inches, seem less. His nose had an inward curve to it and his substantial chin was dark with blue-black stubble.

McCool glared back at Everton, the sudden twitching of whose shoulders disturbed the sleeping man on the stretcher. Vallance blinked himself awake, studied the upper foliage with its myriad strands of linking lianas and then glanced round at his bearers.

'Something up, chaps?' he asked, with mock cheerfulness.

He was ignored. Everton spoke. 'Sorry, sarge. I just saw the funny side of it, that's all. We all know Ginger wants to go on

126

the stage as a ventriloquist or something when the war's over. But mockin' birds in a Burmese jungle seemed a bit farfetched, I thought.'

'Nobody pays you to think, you toffee-nosed git. So shut up,' the NCO admonished him. Turning back to Ahmed, McCool made a big effort to take the agitation out of his scouts. 'Now see 'ere, Ahmed, if that's all that's botherin' you, forget it. Ginger More is a first class bloke. I'd vouch for him anywhere. All he's doin' is indulgin' his 'obby, imitatin' nature an' that. If the slant-eyes 'ear more bird noises than usual it ain't likely to make a whole lot of difference.

'So get back up front an' carry on doin' that great job you started! Chop, chop, off you go!'

The brothers were clearly far from satisfied. Yusuf gnawed his upper lip while Ahmed thumped his turbaned head and again toyed with an earring. Yusuf, the one usually silent, protested.

'But this man, he talks like one full of rice wine, an' that is dangerous, sahib!'

McCool wanted to wave them away,

but he had both hands full. 'Don't be silly, lads, you're over-reactin'. I'll send 'im back shortly when I've finished doin' the orderly stuff!'

Ahmed blinked several times, murmured something to his brother and led him forward again, but the usual spring was out of the Burmese brothers' step, and Britwell was quick to notice this. He had a lot of confidence in the natives. He felt that they would not complain without reason, and Yusuf's few words had intrigued him. The journalist waited a couple of minutes until the scouts were out of earshot. He then overtook the stretcher, nodded to the wounded man and addressed the NCO.

'All right if I go further up the line for a while, sergeant?'

McCool, who was wondering how long he should stay with his stretcher chore before packing it in, scowled at him. He would have liked to suggest that the civvy was poking his nose into military matters again, but he declined to say as much. Instead, he moved his shoulders in a sign of acquiescence.

'I expect it wouldn't be a bad idea, Britwell. Another pair of eyes up front won't do us any harm.'

Scoop patted him lightly on the shoulder and gradually moved up the column. He spoke a word or two of encouragement here and there to men whose faces he knew, trying to put the names to them. With an effort he recollected the names of Littleton, Pierce, Douty and Smith.

Corporal Judd was some seven yards ahead of Lofty Littleton, and the Burmese were moving along side by side, just ahead of the corporal. Ginger More was further ahead still. As Britwell came up with Judd, the redhead stopped his bird imitations and whistled experimentally a few bars of 'John Peel'. He sounded to those nearest behind him to be in a good mood: perhaps too jovial for safety.

'Is Ginger all right, would you say, corporal?'

Mick Judd shortened his pace slightly and glanced sideways at Britwell who noticed a troubled look in the other's brown and green irises.

'I wouldn't know for sure, mate. Ginger

is moody, hard to weigh up. Sometimes he's on top of the world. Other times he's in the dumps. He gave me his Sten about half an hour ago. Took a rifle instead. I don't know if that means anything.'

'The scouts were upset by his bird imitations. They complained to McCool, but he shooed them away. He hadn't finished his stint on the stretcher. Do you happen to know if Ginger has the first aid pack with him?'

'What makes you ask that?' Judd queried, suddenly startled.

'Well, there's a small bottle of medicinal brandy in it. I wondered if he'd tampered with it. One of the Bolis said he sounded as if he was full of rice wine.'

Judd dabbed his neck with a broad square of khaki handkerchief. 'I see what you're gettin' at. I don't rightly recall if he had the pack with him, but I know he has a weakness for the hard stuff. You think he might run us into trouble?'

'That's what the native boys are anticipating. Do you think we could talk some sense into him, seeing the sergeant isn't available?'

'We could try, I suppose, but he's a difficult lad to handle,' Judd commented. 'Let's give it a go.'

Side by side they lengthened their stride again. The Bolis made way for them and clearly approved what they were setting out to do. Nearly five minutes elapsed before they were close enough to speak to the redhead without shouting.

Judd called: 'Ginger, slow up a bit.'

More turned and glanced in their direction. He stopped whistling, giggled and murmured a few words which sounded like ' . . . 'is 'ounds an' 'orn in the mornin'.'

Britwell called after him: 'Ginger, you're getting too far ahead for comfort and you're making too much noise. The scouts are worried about you.'

'Push off, you interferin' civvy, an' take that Cheshire corporal with you!'

Almost running, they came up with him fairly quickly. His glance radiated pure venom as Judd and Britwell flanked him on either side.

'I shouldn't be the one to 'ave to tell you, Britwell, you're supposed to watch an' send back press reports. Fightin' an' fightin' men 'ave nothin' to do with you. Why don't you keep your place as a civvy?'

Judd sniffed. 'You've been 'ittin' the bottle, Ginger, an' you could be puttin' the whole outfit in danger!'

More lashed out with an elbow and caught the corporal in the ribs, winding him. He turned to Britwell, but the latter moved slightly further away.

'You stupid blockhead, More! There's nothing in my terms of reference to say I can't fight with my own countrymen. You're more of a liability just now than the fellow on the stretcher!'

The redhead swore at him and aimed a blow with the stock of his rifle. Britwell avoided it, sidestepped him and helped him on his way. As More hurtled past him, he hit him a hard glancing blow on the angle of the jaw, so that the redhead gained momentum and fetched up hard with his head and shoulders against the unyielding bole of a tree.

'That does it, you interferin' bastard!'

More started to straighten up. He

raised the barrel of the rifle with the intention of using it on his assailant. Judd at once brought up his Sten and pointed it at the redhead's chest.

'That's enough, More! If anyone gives away our position by shootin' the culprit will be me!'

For a few seconds, Britwell was unsure of the outcome. The Bolis came steadily closer, obviously aware of what was going on. More glanced back along the track, gradually calmed himself and stood up.

'All right, we'll settle this later. But *I'm* stayin' in front till Dick McCool relieves me an' that's final. Here, civvy, carry the first aid pack. You might as well do something to earn your keep.'

Britwell caught the pack which was hurled at him. More lowered his shoulder weapon and scampered ahead. Judd straightened up and relaxed his muscles, breathing hard. The Bolis slowed in their approach, their eyes showing sympathy particularly for Britwell.

'Better let him go for now, corporal. I'll drop back and see if McCool will intervene.'

Judd nodded and slowly started forward again. At a sauntering pace, Britwell allowed the others to slowly overtake him. He was reflecting that although the sun owed them several hours of daylight the shadows were already deepening around the tree boles.

He had a premonition that something was about to happen. This made him keep moving forward instead of halting until the stretcher came up. Along with the others near the front he perceived the beginning of another track going off to the left from the one they were using.

A minute or so later, a harsh abrasive cry came from the front of the column. This had the effect of stopping the marching men in their tracks. Many of them recognized the angry voice of More, but his words did not carry very far.

'Bloody 'ell! What sort of an army unit would leave a piece of wire across the track?'

Judd heard the words and guessed at their significance. Fresh perspiration was spurting from his neck and forehead as he stiffened and stopped. More had tripped over a wire. A wire left there for a special purpose. Not by the British, either.

From right ahead and round a small bend in the track, the sinister hollow chatter of a Japanese 'woodpecker' machine gun sounded off. One prolonged burst and then silence. No human cries. Nothing to add to the already killing suspense. Nothing to throw light upon the sudden happening.

Britwell felt his nerves jumping as Judd and the Bolis came hurrying back towards him.

9

At once, the journalist raised both arms and faced those who were still behind him. The Bolis went by him and came to the alternative track in a few yards. At that point, they blocked the track the unit had been using and hurriedly redirected the rear of the column into the other one.

The commandos behind the stretcher hastened forward and came up with the wounded man. McCool, who was tired and a little shaken by the unexpected shooting, turned over the carrying job to Jack and Sam Blade.

'All right, all right, so we take a different route! Trouble right ahead. But what's 'appened? Anybody 'it?'

'You'll have to assume Ginger More has bought it, sergeant,' Britwell told him. 'Any attempt to get along to where he was shot at amounts to suicide!'

'The Japs will be in the thick brush between the two tracks,' Ahmed explained.

'Please, sahib, hurry!'

Led by the natives, the front half of the line went into the new track with the stretcher wobbling along behind them. McCool began to drop to the rear, his feeling for More over-riding his sense of responsibility.

Judd called back to him. 'They were waitin' for us, sarge. Ginger tripped over a wire. It couldn't be helped. Speed it up, can't you? These local lads are the only ones who can get us away.'

'But we can't just leave Ginger without knowin' if 'e's dead or not,' the senior NCO protested.

Britwell's mouth dried out. 'He was liquored up, McCool. He wouldn't stand a chance. Why don't you thank your lucky stars you've only lost one man, and take evasive action while you can? If we don't move soon they could take the lot of us before we get to the river!'

McCool glowered at his adviser, allowed his troubled gaze to fall on the stretcher and its bearers, and then gave in. Fifty yards up the new track, the Bolis barred the way.

Judd murmured: 'All right, Ahmed, I'll buy it. What's your plan?'

'There is just as likely to be an ambush up this track as there was up the other. We must get off this one at once. The going will be easier a little way to the north. You will make the others follow us?'

Judd hesitated for a few seconds, clenched the muscles of his jaw and then nodded. The brothers examined the north side of the track and hurriedly selected a section formed by the bushes known as *bizat*. A short exchange in the Burmese dialect resulted in Yusuf spreading his arms and leaning forward into the bush. At first it did not yield, but when Ahmed severed two or three stems with deft flicks of his *dah*, Yusuf sank slowly down, away from the track, taking the dry dusty foliage with him.

Blowing the tricky dust out of his face, Yusuf implored the soldiers to move forward over his body, while his brother laid about him with a will, slashing this way and that, enlarging the pocket of space beyond the track-side scrub.

Britwell and Judd went forward first. The latter picked up Yusuf's big knife and leaned into the bushes on one side, hacking away at them fiercely to assist Ahmed. The Blades moved clumsily over the outstretched figure and others followed. Weariness soon stopped Judd's effort, but Ahmed worked on until his arms finally tired. He then used his feet and kicked down several thick stems, until a narrow path could be negotiated between more *bizat* and a great oval of bamboo with a sinister skeletal rattle.

Britwell went back and forcibly hauled the last two men over the gap created by Yusuf. He was anxious to see the scout on his feet. Yusuf, equally anxious to rise out of his compromising position, accepted the offer of assistance. Between them, they pushed back the bushes which had been temporarily flattened.

The fascination of knowing that the enemy was so near kept Britwell peering through the trees, but Yusuf, who was fighting a battle not to sneeze, brushed himself down and drew the journalist after him. Britwell responded at once, wondering if the brown flesh of the locals was less susceptive to the irritation caused by the *bizat*. There was no time to ask about it.

In spite of the tiredness occasioned by the wearing mode of jungle travel, the column was moving with a certain amount of spring in its steps. For several minutes there was a bottleneck at the rear of the stretcher, but that soon eased as the sky brightened due to the thinning out of the trees.

Quite soon after that, the whole party began to imagine the small men in jockey caps and rubber boots sprouting out of the trees behind them. The sudden cries of barking wild dogs did nothing to ease their nerves. Britwell and Yusuf hurried forward, breathing hard.

Soon they overtook Ahmed, closely followed by Judd. For a short while, Ahmed seemed without any special sort of a plan, but even his impassive features showed enough emotion to reveal that the party was still threatened.

'Those were wild dogs back there?' Britwell asked.

'Wild dogs of Nippon soldiers, sahib, calling to one another. They are searching for us, even now. We cannot make any speed to the river unless we abandon the man on the stretcher.'

'An' we can't do that,' McCool muttered, having closed up with them.

'How far is the river now, Ahmed?' Britwell persisted.

'About a half mile, in that direction, sahib. But we don't want to head straight for it. If all goes well, there will be a raft hidden about a mile further north. We need a raft to take us over. The river is wide in this area and the current is strong in places.'

'It wouldn't do to get caught half way over by prowling Japs,' Britwell commented.

Before anyone could comment further, a distant high-pitched voice took their attention. It came from the direction of the twin tracks.

'Hey, you British soldiers! Your red-headed friend is looking for you. Come back here. This is Nippon soldier. We want to make friends with you!'

The sweating troopers turned and looked at one another, but kept on going, hoping that the Japanese would not emerge from the thicker jungle until they had opened up a bigger gap. Only McCool looked as if he believed More was still alive.

'They couldn't have missed him with that machine-gun burst, old man,' Vallance remarked from the stretcher.

A little way ahead, Britwell remarked to Ahmed, 'You need someone to divert the enemy, until you find the raft.'

Ahmed nodded and glanced in the direction of his brother. The two Burmese hesitated. Prompted by a sudden knowledge of the desperate nature of the situation, the journalist turned to McCool.

'The Japs could show up almost at any time, sergeant. Someone has to distract them. I'll do it, if you like. Give you time to get to the river with the stretcher.'

McCool argued. 'What do you know about bush warfare an' livin' off the land, Britwell?'

'All right, name your own men to do it, or consider parting with your guides!'

Britwell threw back at him.

McCool hunched his shoulders, wracked by indecision. He glanced back, shook his head, opened his mouth but did not manage to say anything. While he hesitated, four vultures suddenly disturbed, back in the heavy jungle, took off and flew around in small circles, squawking and pecking at each other.

'Go ahead, then, mate. But just remember that you did it all off your own bat. *I* didn't ask you to volunteer.'

Britwell nodded, not knowing why he had pushed himself for so hazardous a task. He moved between the Bolis and explained what he intended to do. Ahmed at once approved, and nodded.

'We shall make a short detour to keep out of sight. We will wait for an hour in case you can catch up with us. If you miss us, you must get across the river at all costs. I will have friendly people on the lookout for you.'

Guide and journalist shook hands. Ahmed raised his arm and pointed in a new direction, where a slight down gradient would afford them temporary cover in a short distance. Britwell stepped aside, aware of a sudden warmth in the regard of the Liverpudlians as they moved past him. Judd edged to the back.

'I don't give much for your chances, chum, but I 'ave to admire your guts. 'Ere, take this Sten. You *will* use it, if you 'ave to?'

Britwell nodded and smiled grimly. 'I'll take steps to keep myself alive, all right. Good luck.'

'An' 'ere's a grenade, in case you 'ave to blast your way clear. Set for four seconds, after the pin's out.'

Britwell handled the proffered explosive gingerly, and thrust it into his shirt. Judd moved off, reluctantly, and Yusuf came running back to hand over a short-handled knife about the size of a bayonet.

'This will be useful, sahib. You can cut a length of bamboo. Slit it, and shake it to make a clatter. It will draw the enemy in your direction. Do not take too many chances.'

'I'd feel better with you with me, Yusuf, but it hasn't to be. Here's hoping it won't be too long before we meet up again.'

At last, the Burmese ran from him, and Britwell angled his hurried walk towards the nearest part of the river. He raised his sun spectacles, studied the shadowed terrain behind him and lengthened his stride.

Five minutes later, he suppressed a cry of surprise as his feet slithered downwards into a hollow.

10

The startled correspondent slithered down ten feet until the slope gave out. His heels had made twin tracks in the fallen leaves. As he squatted breathlessly with his legs drawn up under him he sniffed the smell of decaying foliage and wondered how long it had been since another human had entered the hollow.

He began to think in terms of personal survival.

He had with him his all-purpose pack which contained among other things a writing pad and a supply of pencils. His water canteen was three-quarters full. The Sten had weighed heavily on his arm. One of his trouser pockets bulged with an extra magazine which he hoped he would never have to use. Yusuf's knife was slotted through his belt over his buttocks.

For a time, he wondered why he had offered himself as a human decoy. Was his job, that of recording and reporting, less important than the strike power of McCool's displaced unit? He supposed that it was. Getting out the despatches would be difficult, in the event that he survived. He supposed that his reports could be got out by radio in certain circumstances, but that for the time being high command would be against such a move, in case the broadcast told the enemy too much about their location.

He felt that he had been in the hollow far too long, although only three minutes had elapsed since he made his uncere-monious entry. His heart thumped as he scrambled to the rim again and peered around for signs of the enemy. Fortu-nately, they had not yet appeared.

He scrambled out on the opposite side to which he had entered and headed purposefully towards the east and the river. Caution made him zigzag from one large tree bole to another, in the hope that anyone suddenly finding traces of him would have difficulty in catching sight of his fleeting figure.

A formidable island of bamboo reminded him of Yusuf's advice. He circumnavigated it and paused on the far side, drawing the knife carefully from his belt. He found the stems easy enough to cut down, but his first attempt at cutting a slit was a failure. Having slashed one in half, he took more care with the second one and moved on again before trying out its efficacy.

It was a rattling success. At first he startled himself with the sudden clatter, but soon he was gritting his teeth and shaking it with all his strength. When he desisted, the sound still made his ears ring and nearly a minute had elapsed before the first cries of surprise carried to him.

He made fifty yards of progress, making himself walk slowly. Pigeons and parrots fluttered above the trees, and protesting gibbons removed themselves to a greater distance. He stumbled a time or two as his attention was on the right rather than in front of him.

With his sun spectacles up on his forehead, he probed the gloom for signs of his pursuers. Presently, he saw the first, a short stocky pear-shaped individual who was pointing animatedly but vaguely in his direction.

Giving the bamboo a few more short sharp shakes, he then hurled it away from him and scrambled for cover. Behind a tree bole, he paused and watched. By the time he had glimpsed three men he knew that the Japanese outfit was strung out in a staggered line between his own position and the water. His obvious move was to keep going north, away from them, but that would only put them nearer the main British party and he felt he could not do that.

He wondered briefly if he should abandon his weapons in case they came upon him and depend upon his non-combatant flashes to get him reasonable treatment. He soon concluded, however, that being so far from civilisation the enemy would not concern themselves about rules. Either he would be shot, or he would end up building a railroad along with other unfortunate prisoners.

For a time, he trotted from bole to

bole. This progress was abandoned when he noticed that the pursuers were also trotting and cutting down the distance between them with stunning rapidity.

After this, his heart started to thump. Knowing that he was nearing a crisis in his life, he glanced at his watch. It was nearly half past seven. He had lost count of the date. Visions from the past filled his mind fleetingly. For a time he was with his brother's company in Italy. That gave way to the busy sub-editor's room in Fleet Street.

He checked his thoughts in case they undermined his morale. When the distance between himself and his pursuers was about one hundred yards he went to earth and began to crawl westward, hoping that the extended line of searchers could be outflanked. On his hands and knees he managed about fifty yards. His labouring breath then led him to seek a hiding place.

A stout green bush with shiny leaves seemed to be the solution. He crawled under it with exaggerated care, disturbing two small creatures before he managed to drag his knapsack and Sten in after him. By this time the tension was really playing him up. His heart thumped and his breathing suggested that he had taken part in a marathon race. He breathed with his mouth in a round 'O', hoping that the Japanese would not blunder into him.

Their unintelligible cries came nearer. Most of them were further east than his hiding place. Soon, he was wincing every time they struck at a bush with their weapons. There was a pattern to the muted sounds of their advance. They were still maintaining a line with some ten to fifteen yards between each soldier.

In the last twenty yards or so, his ears were really straining. Just when he thought that all the searchers were east of him, a man grunted. This one was likely to pass within five yards of him on the river side.

Britwell stiffened. Another man with a fruity voice made a comment and chuckled. The speaker was on the other side and probably the furthest out on the flank. For a time, his powers of perception remained clear. Those troopers on the east end of the line appeared to be a few yards ahead of the west end flank. He wondered about that.

And then the present blanked out for a few seconds.

He started to think: *Seven-thirty-five on a pleasant evening early in 1944. Scoop Britwell, war correspondent extraordinary, could go out any time. No more communiques. Lost without trace . . . until intelligence reports pieced together his demise in years to come.*

The soldier on his right passed quite close, but not close enough, burping noisily and muttering to himself. At the crucial time, a sharp word of command came from the right. The searchers halted and exchanged views on where the Englishman had gone to earth. Presently, they started forward again. Britwell's ears told him that the man nearest on the right had resumed, but the one soldier on his left was slow to go forward again.

The latter was reprimanded and he muttered to himself, deliberately dropping behind the others. Insects were beginning to crawl inside the neck of Britwell's shirt, and this irritated him and made him want to emerge at the earliest possible moment. He had developed a chronic fear of leeches and similar creatures.

The sounds of searching men receded. Britwell counted up to thirty and then started to wriggle clear, head first. A sudden patter, as of lightly falling rain puzzled him and made him turn his head. He did so, and at once spotted the man with the fruity voice, who had been answering a call of nature.

At the same time, the Japanese turned and saw him. Not ten yards separated them. Britwell felt trapped. His heightened perceptions weighed everything he could see of the other. The Jap was of average height, with a broad muscular chest, narrow hips and short legs.

As he adjusted his dress and reached for his rifle, his slanted eyes widened with disbelief. His nose was small and flat, the lower part of his cleanshaven face was full. A thick-lipped smile which augured no good showed a prominent set of yellowing upper teeth.

Britwell was surprised that he did not at once call out and give the alarm. He came forward gripping his rifle easily in one hand, the other groping towards the bayonet in his belt. He was actually laughing he was so confident, but his laughter was gusty and unvoiced.

With an effort, Britwell heaved and rolled clear, minus his Sten and the pack. While he was still on his knees, he tossed aside the grenade which he knew he could not use in close combat. The only weapon he had to hand was the Burmese short knife. He wondered if he could get to it without alerting the other.

The Nip soldier's voice sounded a little and then the laughter was at an end. The Oriental toyed with the idea of shooting his victim from close quarters, but that notion did not please him. Instead, he moved closer with the weapon held tightly by the barrel.

'So Engleesh pig, you hide from the soldiers of Imperial Nippon. Have you no courage that you slink about like an animal?'

Rising to his feet, Britwell nodded and cautiously pointed to his shoulder flashes. The broad grin was back on the other's face. From six feet away he suddenly lunged forward and swung the stock of the rifle, using it for a club. Britwell backed hurriedly and avoided the blow, licking his lips and wondering how much time would elapse before the other Japs would become aware of the discovery. He had a feeling that his adversary was something of a sadist, that he would not be permitted to live long enough to concern the others.

Two quick rushes in succession with the rifle swinging this way and that and only missing the target by inches. The Jap perspired and appeared to lose some of his patience. At the third onslaught, Britwell disconcerted him by swinging with an elbow which rather luckily connected with the other's neck.

After that, a certain Oriental deadliness pokered the Jap's face. He adopted the stance of a professional killer and came forward without so much as a flicker in his eyes. This time he telegraphed his rifle swing, watched which way Britwell would jump and then coiled himself up for sudden action. His agility was quite remarkable. Britwell marvelled at it even as the soldier's flying legs came hurtling at him some two feet above the ground.

Taken by surprise, the Englishman could only tense himself and await the shock of the kick. One booted foot connected with his groin and the other struck him low on the thigh, knocking him over backwards and starting the first of a series of intense shooting pains from the abdomen.

Britwell landed on his back, winded and pained. In spite of his injuries, his back was still full of feeling. The handle and blade of Yusuf's knife pressed into it and dug a couple of vertebrae.

For a second or so, the fallen man was unaware of his assailant's actual position. In fact, the Jap's spirited foot attack had carried him on beyond his victim. He rolled easily to his feet, breathing strongly and wearing his asinine grin at full stretch.

Britwell levered an elbow under himself

and stared at him. He was shifting his weight onto the other arm and groping round behind him when the Jap leisurely toyed with the lanyard of a whistle which was looped round his neck.

The Oriental decided against blowing the alarm. Instead, he discarded his rifle, unfastened the top two buttons of his tunic, adjusted his jockey cap and casually prepared to leap upon his victim and do what he had to do by brute force.

Britwell waited with his eyes half-closed. He recollected briefly how he had answered Mick Judd about using his weapons if he had to. He thought of that other time in Italy when he had taken an active part in a successful attempt to cross a defended bridge. Now, he was about to become a combatant again, only this time it was a matter of survival. The jungle law prevailed.

Like a rugby forward hurling himself for the line to score a try the ruthless Japanese sprang. His arms were bent, his hands so arranged that he could make a sudden clutch at the throat on arrival. Britwell's mouth dried out afresh. He rolled two feet to one side, hauled out the knife and clenched his fist about the handle, pointing the sharp two-sided blade.

Hot breath came at his face. The hairy-backed hands reached for his throat. The Jap's pupils appeared to dilate. And then the point of the knife entered his body at the base of the thorax, below the sternum.

The weight of the assailant drove in the blade up to the hilt. Britwell's upraised right shoulder caught the other high on the chest, jerking the head forward. Saliva flew from the wide mouth. The Jap's strength began to ebb at once. The eyes opened like a cat's, looked troubled and then started to close and mist over.

Britwell heaved himself clear. He was unprepared for the long cry of agony which went up so close to him. He stood up, his legs unsteady, his hands on his hips and his mind busy. His first move was to get back to the bush where he had taken shelter. He hauled out his knapsack and the Sten gun, feeling quite sure that he would have to use it.

Groping under the bush made him breathless again. He was on his knees with the Sten cradled in his arms when he spotted the two nearest Jap troopers. They were about forty yards away. Some trick in the erratic distribution of trees made the two parties visible to one another. As one Jap pointed to him for the benefit of the other, he rose stiff-legged, pointed the automatic weapon and squeezed the trigger.

The vibration, a new sensation with him, went through him. He panned the muzzle around and had the satisfaction of hitting one man who was seeking to aim at him and the other as he was diving for cover. There were lots of shouts from the river end of the line, but no return of fire.

Britwell sniffed. He recovered his grenade and returned to the body of his victim. Mindful of what had been done with Ronnie Peyton's lifeless body he was in a mood to retaliate. Discarding the Sten, he dragged the Japanese to the base of the concealment bush, heaved the legs and hips under it and gingerly tinkered with the grenade.

It was not difficult to bury it in an upright position in the soft earth under the bush. The most ticklish bit was fixing the whistle lanyard to the pin. His fingers were a little unsteady, but he managed it and withdrew. Without knowing quite why, he removed the Jap's jockey cap, tried it on for size and then thought about withdrawal.

Grabbing the knapsack and the Sten, he hurled the Jap's rifle muzzle first into a bush. It was high time to be moving. The rest of the platoon was on its way back. This far, the fact those nearest the river were furthest away had worked in his favour.

His intention now was to go east, behind the line of retreating searchers. He moved off, wondering if his luck would hold.

11

Some time after eight o'clock in the evening; blundering eastward through what seemed to be linked patches of formidable scrub. Conscious of the growing shadows due to the bunched foliage high above him. No time to look down at his watch in case he was observed before he had a chance to duck down.

Every now and then a chattering gibbon would attract his attention as it swung further away from the line of his movements.

No Japs as yet. No reaction from the spot where he had left the dead man. Nothing at all to betray the position of the enraged searching soldiers. No sign of a brief lightening of the sky ahead, suggesting that the river was close. Nothing. All negative.

The breath coming in short sharp gasps, the legs aching with his protracted efforts to move clear of danger over the yielding jungle surface. Occasionally, the barking of a deer, and one time the ferocious growling of a prowling jungle cat.

In seeking to maintain his progress in the intended direction, he had to weave in and out of the bushes and bamboos. After a time, he began to have doubts as to whether he was still moving eastward, or whether he had unconsciously changed direction to north-east or south-east.

Uncertainty made his stomach crawl. The words of McCool about his lack of training in jungle warfare and survival were brought home to him. The jungle was neutral. He did not know enough to read any natural signs which might suggest he was on the right route.

All he could do was keep on and hope for the best, which at this moment in time could only amount to prolonged survival. No let up, no relaxation. Only the will to go on, indefinitely. He saw with absolute clarity how the jungle tapped a man's character to the depths, how it sorted out his every weakness and sometimes discovered hidden strengths.

Even darkness would provide a doubtful advantage. All he could do was head for water and hope that friendly forces would be on the lookout. Water . . . the contents of his water canteen were swishing about this way and that. His acute hearing was trying to put music to the sounds of its gyrations when the distant *crunch*! of the grenade exploding blasted him out of a growing sense of nightmare.

He stopped suddenly, turned in a flat-footed jump to face the direction of the sound, and grimaced. Now, he knew things. He knew for instance that the prowling Japs had discovered the body, and that their efforts to retrieve it from the bush had caused the grenade to go off.

He also had a good idea of the distance between the searchers and himself. Tree boles and thick foliage had a way of distorting sound effects, but he felt reasonably pleased with the apparent distance between himself and his pursuers. Furthermore, he had a means by which to check his own direction. And that certainly helped.

As near as he could judge he had deviated a little towards the north-east, but not appreciably so. He bent down and marked the direction of the big bang with the barrel of the Sten, and then he started to relax. The mind was functioning again. He started to calculate. Two to three hours of daylight: a river which ought to be no more than a furlong away at the nearest point.

If the area was devoid of people he had a rather long trek ahead of him, along the river bank. Direction, north. Another batch of problems. A man working the bank of a *chaung* was likely to be observed at times by watchers on the other side. He glanced up into the liana-draped treetops and decided that the jungle was more desirable than some Burmese locations.

Two mouthfuls of water from the canteen, and then on again. Caution reminded him that not all of the Jap squad were necessarily as far away as the scene of the grenade explosion. He went warily, but with confidence in his sense of direction. No green-clad Jap came up on his left and his thoughts were busy with speculation about the village of Daung Bazar. 'The Market of the Hill Village'. Houses on stilts, and sad-looking thin hill cattle, and gracefully moving attentive Burmese maidens prepared to do anything to keep the British soldiers in the remote fastnesses of their country.

He sighed and wondered if in fact there was anything really attractive for the wanderer, other than the overpowering physical beauty of the scenery.

★   ★   ★

The river which barred his path some minutes later had been in his thoughts for so long that in a way it was a bit of anticlimax. It had a grey swollen look about its surface as the currents carried its promising volume steadily southward. Not a river to swim in for any length of time, or to cross by swimming power alone, unless the current nearer the centre was less powerful.

Britwell cautiously slid down a narrow gully until his boots were just touching the lapping water. With the Sten on one side of him and his pack on the other, he placed his hands behind his head and tried to relax himself while his eyes were busy. When he was trying hard to penetrate the gloom beyond the farther bank a marauding flight of mosquitoes settled around his head, obviously thinking seriously about making a meal off him.

With a casualness which surprised him, he swept off the jockey cap (which he had forgotten he was wearing) filled it with water and slopped the whole lot over his head and neck before replacing it. He knew from experience that anopheles mosquitoes were very difficult to dissuade, but on this occasion they suddenly lost interest in him and moved on.

No promising signs of life on the further bank. One or two amphibious creatures sported in and out of the water in an inlet, and a little further south three small brown men in the traditional Burmese cotton costume were working like ants, drawing out of the water one of the natives' dugout canoes.

Before he had proper time to consider whether to try and attract attention across the river — a furlong in width at that point — the boatmen and their craft had disappeared from view.

Britwell withdrew from the water's edge. He rested for a while longer, digesting a couple of bananas and part of a cocoanut which he had collected on his way east. He had reason to be thankful that he had a strong stomach, one which could easily adjust itself to an entirely new diet.

McCool and the others were in his thoughts when he started the long walk north in an effort to rejoin them.

★　★　★

Dusk. Nearly three hours after the sharp confrontation with the Japanese soldier. It seemed more like three years as the solitary man stood under a tree a few feet back from the bank and looked across the river's black surface.

Dusk was of remarkably short duration. And yet it had proved long enough for Britwell to make a useful discovery. He was grinning in the dark, although his trials of the day were yet far from over.

He had the feeling that his left leg was shorter than his right: a feeling due to the amount of work he had done on the side of the *chaung*, sometimes in the water and sometimes out of it. Slithering along the slippery banks with the added weight of the gun and his pack.

Twice he had entered the water. The first time it had merely been a matter of wading up to the thighs, but the second time a sudden caterwauling of animals and birds had made him think moving Japs were close in the vicinity. On that occasion, he had precipitately launched himself up to his neck.

Mindful of the coolness of the night in those latitudes, he had walked himself dry and warm again in the last hour in the vain hope that he would not have to enter the water again to make the big crossing.

His grin, in fact, was wolfish. The legs which had once supported him as a cross-country runner had stood up to the rigours of Burma this far very well. He supposed that his special sort of tiredness had something to do with being entirely alone and having to move in a constant state of vigilance.

There was just this one thing which had fanned his hopes. At that moment it was dangling above his head from a bunch of plaited liana. Ronnie Peyton's camera. Someone had decided to leave it hanging there from the bough above to indicate the spot at which the raft had departed. A friendly sign. Enough to make a despondent man dredge up some more energy to add companionship to his state of survival.

It never occurred to Britwell that the object might have been stolen or lost and rigged to blow him apart, or to betray him. Besides, out there upon the waters he had heard sounds which led him to believe that the squat raft was on its way across: that the rest of the outfit with which he had dropped from the skies had delayed their water crossing until nearly dusk.

Dusk was almost total darkness as he cut down the camera with the borrowed knife. At his back, the jungle was close, dense and alive with the perpetual sound of moving insects. Across the other side, the same sort of sounds prevailed, but they were muted.

In spite of his recently boosted hopes, Britwell had a lot to do. He could hardly expect the raft to put back for him, and any loud calling might bring undesirables down upon his friends and himself. He kept reminding himself that divine providence, or the devil's own luck, or a combination of both, had been necessary to keep him out of the clutches of the enemy in the previous few hours.

He thought about whistling. Even as he considered it, he felt again — in his imagination — the breath of the Japanese soldier who had intended to strangle him. And the impact when their bodies had met. He shuddered, thought again about whistling, and licked his lips.

He cupped his hands to his mouth for his first attempt at 'D'ye ken John Peel', and although he kept well to the tune, his whistling did not carry. In desperation, he tried again, whistling louder and keeping going until he had rendered the tune to a whole verse. In the ensuing silence, he heard voices again. Somewhere in the opaque blackness British soldiers were talking to one another, possibly about him and his imagined fate.

His spirits sank slowly. They had not heard and they were still going away from him. He would have to take to the water and hope to catch up with them. The hazards appalled him. He hoped nothing would go wrong with this desperate venture. The waterway had broadened as he stumbled north to this point. At no time had he any reason to think that the current had abated.

He groaned, took a few deep breaths and stepped cautiously forward down the slope. He imagined that the water temperature was much lower than when he had plunged in earlier. Reason told him a marked drop was unlikely, but that same reason did nothing to boost his spirits.

Foot by foot he went down, until he

was up to his neck. He had a water canteen strap and the carrying strap of the camera looped around his neck. The Sten and the pack were draped rather uncomfortably across his back.

His first strokes were tentative and exploratory. He used the breast-stroke for his big effort. All went well for the first five minutes. He made steady progress without knowing how the strong current was taking him downstream. He felt that he was moving in a south-easterly direction.

He imagined Japs forming up on the bank behind him as the water slopped about his ears. Some time later, he turned onto his back. At once, he was in difficulties. Something was tugging at his neck, trying to drag him down. In the dark, it was a moment for panic. It took a few seconds to discover that it was the camera causing the trouble.

The camera itself had caught on some underwater obstruction: probably a sub-merged tree, the branch of which protruded upwards. For more than half a minute, he struggled to keep his head above water, and then he managed to slip the strap over his head and obtain relief.

As he panted for breath, the weight of the Sten threw him out of balance. Holding onto the camera, as he was, he knew a moment of panic. He gritted his teeth, yanked the offending instrument really hard and felt it come away from whatever had been holding it.

Coughing on tepid river water, he almost choked. Without waiting for further complications, he put up the Sten and fired off two short bursts, capsizing himself as he did so. When he came up again, the worst was over.

'Ahoy, there, you on the raft! This is Britwell! Throw me a rope or something, I'm in difficulties!'

A tiny wavelet found his mouth as he uttered the last word, but he heard someone call 'Scoop' and knew that his call for assistance would be answered.

12

The rope snaked across the floundering swimmer almost at once. Britwell grabbed it with both hands, contented himself with treading water, and was slowly hauled alongside of the bulky raft.

Hands reached down to haul him in. As he was levered up the side his probing eyes recognized Yusuf, Everton and Judd. They turned him onto his chest, relieved him of his pack, the Sten and the camera. Next, the canteen was hauled out and finally himself.

McCool called from the far side of the vessel, obviously ill at ease. 'What kept you all this time, Britwell? And why did you 'ave to blast off like that?'

The journalist coughed. 'The camera was caught on an underwater obstruction. After all I've done for you today, I figured I was entitled to some assistance.'

Britwell turned over and sat down, surrendering the knife to Yusuf, its rightful owner. Everton knelt near him, drying off the Sten gun and doing all he could to make sure that it was still in working order.

'You fooled the Japs, then,' Judd murmured. 'Are they still followin' you?'

Britwell nodded. Yusuf patted him on the shoulder and went back to take charge of the second of two long poles, used for propelling the raft.

'So far as I know,' Britwell murmured. 'I had to tangle with one of them before I could get through their line and draw them off.'

'Sure, sure, Everton reckoned 'e 'eard a Sten bein' fired some hours ago, but we thought it must 'ave been a wood-pecker,' Judd replied, with enthusiasm. 'We thought you'd 'ad it. So you fired off a few shots in anger, then?'

'I told you I would, if it was a matter of survival. Yusuf's knife accounted for a big fellow who fancied himself as a wrestler. I used the Sten on two men who were too close for comfort, and the grenade must have accounted for another couple when they found the wrestler's body.'

Judd chuckled to himself, and gave Britwell a playful thump on the shoulder. 'Some non-combatant you turned out to be! After this we'll be able to blackmail you over bein' a combatant!'

'You're assuming we survive and get back to England,' Britwell pointed out.

As soon as he had said the words, he wished he hadn't. There was a lot of fight left in the unit and pessimism had no place on this raft full of purposeful beings.

He added: 'Don't take any notice of me, Juddy. I'm feeling a bit sorry for myself. I'm damned glad to be back with you boys. Believe me, that jungle is a mighty lonely place at night, especially when all you have to think about is the enemy.'

For a minute or two, the raft continued to make slow progress across the powerful waterway. The Boli brothers used their muscular shoulders on the long poles while two commandos assisted them with paddles. Progress was slow. Britwell was wringing out his wet clothes when the next surprise occurred.

Everton cleared his throat and snapped

his fingers a couple of times. 'If we could 'ave a little bit of 'ush, sarge, I think I just 'eard something!'

Such a suggestion from a man renowned for his keenness of hearing and night vision amounted to an order which needed no backing from the senior NCO. Everton's attention was concentrated downstream. Within a minute, several men were able to confirm what their comrade had heard.

'Well?' McCool prompted, in a fierce-whisper.

'A motorboat downstream, comin' closer,' Everton murmured.

All forward progress on the raft had been halted. The Bolis hung onto their poles with their arms crossed and rigid. They looked like dark motionless carved figures. Presently, their heads moved as though they were communicating new anxieties to each other.

Judd remarked: 'We 'ave to assume it's one of theirs.'

No sooner had he spoken than the dark void of blackness further south brightened. The engine noises swelled as though someone had turned up the volume. A cone of light pierced the gloom on the east side of the river and slowly swung around from east to west.

Its source was the deck of a motorboat, for a time out of sight beyond a slight bend. Everyone on the raft ducked down flat, instinctively. Slowly, the beam was panned round, creeping towards the raft and passing over it with maddening slowness. Only the two poles were sticking up, angled almost to vertical.

Britwell peered this way and that as the probing light revealed details in a distorted circle. He guessed from what he saw that the raft was two-thirds of the way across: that over one hundred yards still separated them from the further bank. If the powered boat kept on its present course, it would be upon them long before they could make the bank. Someone had to make a sudden decision. The journalist wondered if McCool was up to it. He crawled to whisper to him.

'What's your plan, McCool? You'll have to wipe them out, otherwise they'll do the same to all of us.'

'What do you reckon?' the NCO asked,

drumming with his fingers on the stock of the other Sten.

'Keep still, and out of sight for as long as possible. Then hit them with what you've got. Stens and grenades it'll have to be. You'll need to hit the searchlight and any guns they have on deck.'

The beam of light had crossed the whole of the river and become diffused amid the packed trees back from the west bank. Already Everton could make out the bows with his naked eyes. McCool licked his dry lips. There was no time to argue tactics.

'All right, lads. Stand to. Don't make a move until *I* do. After that, use everything. No 'alf measures. No quarter. Stens, rifles, grenades, the lot. Go for the light an' the deck guns first!'

No more than fifty yards away, the upper works of the motor launch could be picked out in the slight reflected light of the searchlight. It was mounted not on the deck, but about midships on top of the cabin. Forward, a light-weight gun on a tripod was clearly illuminated with a Jap crouched in the harness behind it. A second gunner hovered behind him with extra belts of ammunition.

The crew had heard the earlier firing of the Sten, and were primed for action. A pair of heavy machine guns flanked the vessel, one to port and one to starboard, lower and wide of the searchlight. There was probably another gun of a similar calibre to the one in the bow right aft. Twelve to twenty personnel. A formidable outfit for eighteen men on a packed, scarcely manoeuvrable raft.

Gradually, the searchlight beam swung back towards the low-lying craft. It was not more than ten yards away when McCool went into action. His first burst splintered the lens and the lamp. After that, all hell was let loose over the small area.

Plunged into sudden darkness, men of both sides plied their weapons. Hoarse shouts from the motorboat's cockpit were drowned in the harsh cacophony of automatic weapons. Two or three of the commandos' weapons were trained on the powered boat's forward gun, but in the blinding darkness they were off their aim for a few vital seconds.

In that time, the rating manning the bow gun went into action. He profited by the raft's lack of movement and his shooting was accurate. A sudden burst of small shells ripped across the centre of the raft before anyone could reply. The area of the occupied stretcher and the immediate deck space surrounding it took a sudden lethal beating. Cries of anguish were drowned.

Understandably, some soldiers threw themselves sideways to avoid being ploughed up by the rush of shells. Judd, armed with the Sten loaned to Britwell, did a quick roll to one side and his gun slipped out of his grasp.

Britwell was startled when the formidable weapon slithered along the uneven surface of the deck and lodged against his thigh.

McCool's voice was hoarse. ''It 'em! What are you waitin' for? Grenades, for Chrissakes, we'll be run down in a minute!'

Two figures moved to a kneeling position, tugging grenades out of their pouches. One after another, Littleton and Thompson released their missiles. Anxiety prompted by the shells and the closing of the vessel to twenty yards spoiled their aim. One grenade exploded two yards wide of the starboard beam at water level. The other erupted while still in the air over the port beam.

Only a second separated the explosions. The unmistakable smell permeated the air. The blinding white light tinged with orange illuminated momentarily and then expunged the advancing boat. The blast of the explosives threatened to tear the prostrate men off the raft.

On came the craft. It was clear to everybody on the raft that a ramming was imminent. Too close for any further grenade throws. Britwell saw the action as though it was in slow motion. The sharp bow creamed towards them, scything through the dark waters like a knife.

The forward Jap gunner loomed steadily higher and more formidable as he struggled to aim his weapon at the low angle. Britwell shook himself, aimed the Sten and fired a short burst. Bullets clanged off the metal frame supporting the gun and then the gunner himself was hit and falling backwards towards the port side.

Five yards short of the collision, Britwell threw himself sideways. He slithered, and the Sten went free for the second time. He stayed down, extending his body to its full length along one of the vast timbers of the raft.

''Old on! Grab everythin'!'

The hoarse voice was unmistakably that of McCool, shouting just on the eve of the shock. The bows hit the corner of the raft with a dull thud. A sudden creaking and splintering of lighter timbers occurred as the stem of the powered craft caved in against the tree bole. The motor launch appeared to back off immediately upon impact. Its engines raced and then it came on again, sheering away and scraping its starboard side slowly along its length at water level.

To those who looked up, the small vessel of war appeared to dwarf the raft until the starboard quarter finally scraped clear and it continued its interrupted journey upstream. There was a shadowy silhouette in the cockpit. Two other figures raced for the starboard machine-gun and hastened to train it as raft and boat moved apart.

Britwell's gritted teeth jarred as the two Stens fired upwards from behind him with seconds to spare. Twin streams of bullets converged upon the gun mounting. The two Japanese ratings, caught in the fusillade of fire, lost momentum. Their movements were punctuated by the bullets striking them.

One slipped over the side, liberally stitched with bullets, while the other collapsed and fell flat behind the gun. Everton and McCool, the Sten gunners, slowly rose to their feet, firing bursts along the launch's water line.

In between bursts, Britwell yelled: 'Look out for the stern gun!'

A kneeling figure, that of Corporal Judd, nudged Britwell, and murmured: ''Ere, cop this, mate!'

Scoop found himself holding a hand grenade for the second time that day. He felt it over in the dark and moved further away from Judd, who had another ready in his hand. The Stens were stunningly silent.

'Any time now, mate!' Judd prompted.

Britwell pulled his pin, started to count and brought back his arm. The semi-circular frame surrounding the after gun swung into view. The gunner's arms groped upwards as he strove to keep his body out of the line of fire. Five yards clear and the gap still widening. It was not clear whether the launch was being steered, or picking its own course.

Suddenly, Britwell aimed his lethal handful and ducked. His face was still turned in the direction of his aim as it exploded aft of the cockpit in the well deck. Another blinding flash, but Judd was not deterred. His grenade burst a foot or two wide of the stern while still in the air. It demolished the rail, the gun and the unfortunate man crouching below it.

Seconds later, several commandos were on their feet. The Sten gunners emptied their magazines into the water line of the receding launch while three grim-faced soldiers hurled grenades into the cockpit. The blast and sudden brightness of the first was immediately followed by the others.

The cockpit appeared to be on fire. No one was firing back. The boat headed on a curving course towards the west bank. Some twenty yards further on, a small internal explosion preceded a greater one which literally blew the craft apart.

The bow and stern ends parted and small debris was still flying through the air as the stern followed the stem to the bottom. A creaming spreading cauldron of angry water formed up over the vessel's last resting place.

The raft was lifting and rocking violently as McCool called his men to order and attempted to take stock of his losses. Britwell met Ahmed at the corner which had received the buffeting. Some of the holding ropes had parted and a gap of a few inches had been opened up. Otherwise, the solid craft was intact.

Ahmed said: 'This time we were lucky, sahib. I am glad you got back to us before the clash. We have lost one of the long poles, perhaps you will help us by paddling.'

Britwell warmly gripped the Burmese by the arm, and accepted the paddle, settling down to do his bit by the weakened corner. Ahmed positioned himself at the forward end on the same side, while his brother worked manfully on the long pole on the opposite side.

Between one hundred and one hundred and fifty yards had been lost due to the current by the time the Boli brothers had restored order and resumed. Whispered bits of information were traded about the raft as the soldiers calmed down and began to think more calmly about what had happened.

Everton moved over to Britwell's side and brought him up to date.

'I don't figure we're goin' to need the stretcher any more in a 'urry, chum. Poor old Jerry Vallance bought it when that forward gun opened up. An' to think we carried 'im all this way, only for that to 'appen.'

'Is he, was he badly knocked about, Everton?'

'Yer, you wouldn't want a close look at 'im. 'E took it right across the chest from one 'ip to the other shoulder. Like a red sash, it looks. Two of our buddies went at the same time. Smithy an' Douty. They both lived up Crosby way. I suppose if they 'ad to go they would 'ave preferred to go together. Makes you wonder what war is all about, though, don't it? An' what it all adds up to. Me, I'm fair sick at times. No wonder they call this outfit the forgotten army.'

Britwell nodded. 'Three more men who won't even get to see Daung Bazar. I know how you feel. This sort of thing, happening in the back of nowhere, makes a man a fatalist, don't you think?'

Everton had heard the term fatalist before. Now, he had a better idea of what it really meant. He stared at Britwell, a man who had not come into the jungle to fight and wondered what the recent events had done to him, whether his normal decent feelings had been seriously impaired.

'I think I know what you mean, chum. You always seem to make sense to me.

'Ello, the east bank ain't far off. Can't say it means an awful lot to me, though. East or west, what's the difference?'

Britwell shrugged. He could have said that perhaps hope lay on the east bank, but he refrained. He was thinking about an old saying his mother used to use. 'East, west, home's best.' But this was no time or place to utter anything that could make a fighting man homesick.

13

'Docking' on the other side was a slow process.

As soon as the action was over, the survivors on the raft appeared to run out of energy. Even the Boli brothers seemed to be drained as they coaxed the craft across the remaining part of the stream and studied the bank for a suitable place in which to put the squat craft ashore.

Two or three men began to doze, even though they were sitting in awkward cross-legged positions. Everton considerately took over Britwell's paddle and afforded the latter a little freedom. He crossed the tree boles, slowly and carefully, studied briefly the covered bodies of the dead, and then lined himself up alongside of Ahmed.

'Is it important where we actually land, Ahmed?'

'Yes, sahib. It is if we want to draw the whole raft clear of the water and leave it out of sight. We are looking for a place where there is a sizeable gap between the trees. Once we find it, all will be well.'

The intensity of the cold was striking through the British. After the heat of the day and the nerve-shattering action, all of them felt under par. Ten minutes dragged by before Yusuf called and pointed. Ahmed approved of the place, and the pair called for a big effort to push the raft in speedily. With one pole and two paddles, it was not an easy task, but as soon as the commandos realized what was afoot several volunteers slipped into the water and began to hold and drag the precious craft inshore.

All fifteen fit men worked hard, using ropes and nearby tree trunks in the hauling process. They were breathless and ready to throw themselves down for rest by the time the raft was sufficiently far up the bank to camouflage it with palm fronds. In a small hollow, a fire was lighted.

McCool approved a fifteen minute stand-down, during which time tea was brewed and cigarettes were smoked. The two Burmese sat easily among the soldiers, their senses alert, and their minds upon the immediate problems to be dealt with that night.

''Ow long will it take us to get to your village, Ahmed?' McCool asked, talking round a cigarette butt.

The Burmese sighed and grimaced. 'It will be some time tomorrow, sahib. We have to cross a busy road used by the Japanese, and then our route is up hill. Probably, tomorrow afternoon.'

McCool nodded, 'All right, then. We'll make a meal, work out some night watch keepin', an' get some sleep. We'll bury our dead at daylight. Does that sound reasonable?'

Ahmed and Yusuf almost chorused their approval. It was clear to Britwell that they had gone up in the general estimation of the soldiers during the time when he had been away from the party.

★ ★ ★

All through the night, the encroaching noises of jungle life formed a sound back-cloth to the resting party. With dawn, the sounds subtly changed. This, combined with the slight rise in temperature, brought the soldiers to wakefulness without any special effort.

Breakfast was a sketchy affair. Corporal Judd finished his food quickly and received permission from a troubled McCool to form a burial party. The Burmese were consulted as to where the burying should be done, and the commandos worked in groups of four to dig out the communal grave. Two parties did the actual digging and a third finished the job of filling in when the bodies had been interred. McCool read a few prayers from a small book which he had been carrying about with him for years. He made a reasonable job of his task, but the overall burial was a sad, depressing occasion which dampened their spirits for the first hour of snake column travel towards the east.

Towards ten in the morning, a gap in the trees ahead, while they were on a downgrade, revealed a long cloud of dust across their path. The leaders at once stopped and those following behind closed up with them and bunched out into a nervous speculative group of observers.

Britwell and Everton, who had been in the rear, were the last to join the crowd. As they did so, the distant sound of heavy lorries on the move drifted towards them.

Ahmed lined up alongside of Britwell, to satisfy his curiosity.

'It is a convoy of Japanese lorries moving south from the area off the meadow where the airstrip was to be, sahib.'

Britwell nodded. 'Where are they heading for, would you say?'

'A few miles further south there is a railhead, which is being extended all the time. They use it to bring up munitions from Mandalay. The enemy is very active in the Shan states.'

'An' your village is on the other side?' Everton queried unnecessarily.

Ahmed nodded very definitely. 'We shall have to take our chances in crossing the road. It will be difficult. If we are seen, we could lead the enemy to our people, with disastrous consequences.'

Britwell got the point at once. He had found himself wondering what sort of British influence had provided these loyal Burmese with their command of English and their sharp grasp of the essentials of jungle warfare. He speculated that they were in for a few major surprises in the village of Daung Bazar, if and when they arrived there.

Thirty minutes later, they were lying prone in cover along the west side of the dirt road, anxiously looking up and down it and wondering what their chances were of crossing it undetected. On the far side, the going was uphill for about a quarter of a mile with waist-high cover of elephant grass, fern and stunted shrubs.

They had reached a critical part of their journey. Everyone felt insecure. It was possible that some of the unsettling feelings would be minimised if they received a good reception in the hill village. No one deigned to speculate openly.

Yusuf came back from the north where he had been making a one-man reccy to try and ascertain how soon the next convoy of trucks was likely to be arriving in their vicinity.

'More lorries in a few minutes,' he announced breathlessly. 'After that, I think we must dash across and get away from the road as quickly as we can.'

McCool untied his handkerchief sweatband from his forehead as he received the information. 'I wish I knew if we should attempt to shoot up the last of the lorries,' he muttered.

Yusuf looked horrified and Ahmed gnawed his full underlip.

'All right, all right,' McCool went on. 'No need to protest. I know it could bring a bloody Jap company down on our backs. All the same, this is furtive work for a commando unit. I reckon desert warfare 'as spoiled us for this sort of activity. So let's bunch up an' be ready. 'Ere they come.'

The first of four lorries, laden with green-clad slant-eyed troops, took what seemed like an age to come into view to the north. Their thick tyres were throwing up waves of dust as they rocked this way and that, moving at a fairly high speed.

The watching men crouched still lower, marvelling at this close view of Imperial Nippon's so-called invincible ground troops. A bespectacled NCO with black tufts of hair on his cheekbones sat impassively beside the driver with his attention wholly on the route ahead.

The canvas coverings had been rolled up at the sides so that the upper trunks of the Jap infantry were clearly visible to the British observers who were only a few yards away. One man with a big jowl was chewing nuts and throwing the shells high over his shoulder, clear of the vehicle.

A second truck quickly followed the first. As that one withdrew a lanky soldier spat over the tailgate and watched his spittle sizzle in the dust. A third and a fourth followed, looming suddenly big and clear through the curtain of dust and putting up a further cloud which soon drifted wide of the road and teased the sensitive nostrils of the British.

The commandos started to tense themselves. Suddenly, McCool was standing up in their midst. He raised his left arm, made a forward gesture with his hand, and stepped forward. The others matched him for speed and movement. No one needed a second bidding. The road was only a few yards wide, but already a subconscious fear of being isolated from one's own kind had affected their attitude towards their present activities.

Side by side, Scoop and Everton sprang clear of the dust and hurled themselves into the fringe of rock and scrub on the other side. Quickly, the party sorted itself out. McCool, sided by Ahmed, led the way up the slope with his broad back bent between his half moons of perspiration.

About fifty yards up the slope there was a small clearing. In it, the NCO paused and watched his men, one by one, as they went by him. It was something he had heard Brigadier Wingate often did. A trick worth copying, if it put heart into the troops.

'There's a lot of loose soil on this slope, lads, so Ahmed says. Be careful 'ow you put your feet down an' try not to dislodge any loose stones. A small landslide could be a disaster to us. I don't want to leave any more of you be'ind like Douty, Smithy an' the paratroop bloke. An' keep in single file, all the time!'

As he issued his last instruction, he sounded really fierce. So much so that Britwell and Everton studied his features and wondered what particular part of the day's stresses were bothering him most. McCool saw six men on their way behind Ahmed. He then stepped into line and encouraged the others to follow him without delay.

Britwell hunkered down, knowing that a minute or so would go by before he could take up his position at the tail of the column. Everton dropped on one knee and began to tease out of the fertile ground one or two roots suitable for chewing. Britwell's gaze was downhill. He studied what he could see of the dust-shrouded road and wondered what it was like further north and south.

Unconsciously, he stood up and gazed back in the direction from which they had come.

Everton murmured: 'I'm beginnin' to

get used to you in that Jap cap, Scoop. What with that an' your sun specs, you've changed your appearance quite a bit since we crash-landed. What are you thinkin' about now?'

'I'm thinking about how the jungle greenery seems to camouflage everything. Right now, I can't see anything to indicate where that river was. Nothing at all. I'm beginning to wonder just how much the Jap reconnaissance planes can pick out from above.'

The Blade brothers and Tufty Pierce moved into line as the distant sound of a powerful engine broke in upon the conversation. For a short time the local foliage put the direction of the new sound in some doubt. Presently, Everton and the journalist pinned it down at the same time.

'Another vehicle coming from the north, Everton. What do you make of it?'

The stocky soldier, who had been a motor mechanic in peacetime, did not give the sort of answer which was expected of him.

'If I didn't think it was impossible, I'd

say that was the sound put up by a British jeep. Is it possible, do you think?'

Britwell slowly shook his head. He respected Everton for the keenness of his senses, but he did not see how a single British jeep could suddenly appear in the midst of Japanese traffic on an occasion like this. Soldier and civilian, both hurriedly aware of the excessive speed of the approaching vehicle, gripped each other.

Before they had the time to step clear of the exposed patch of ground the jeep appeared below them. A bulky officer, probably a Colonel or the equivalent, sat beside the driver. In the back, partially hidden under a net laced with palm fronds, were four others.

The Colonel raised a hand and pointed. Steam was issuing from the radiator. The driver slammed on his brakes, causing the jeep to slither to a sliding halt in a positive curtain of brown dust.

Everton patted Britwell on the shoulder. 'What did I tell you, mate? A British jeep captured by the Japs! I could pick out the sounds of that engine anywhere!'

They were both peering down the slope when the new dust cloud suddenly faded. A junior officer seated on the far side of the truck glanced up the slope and saw them. Britwell reacted instantly, pushing Everton down out of sight. He drew himself up to attention, saluted the party below, got a response and then moved into cover.

'Pass the word forward, chum. Japs below. Keep down and keep moving!'

The Japanese jockey cap had served a useful purpose. For several minutes, the stumbling party expected to hear a sharp word of command from the road, but no one challenged their right to be on the slope. They carried on, their hearts thumping.

* * *

Late in the afternoon, when excessive heat had dulled their alertness, the party felt stones under their feet. They were walking on a path rendered solid with a hard surface. Ahead of them was a gentle

202

murmur of native voices. The Bolis increased their pace while the British felt over their weapons and prudently slowed down.

Within minutes they were entering a wide compound, lined by twin rows of stilted huts topped with palm leaves. Chickens scurried this way and that, underfoot. Two grey-white cows with their ribs showing solemnly watched their approach, munching stolidly on cud.

Everton sniffed as though he had a head cold as his nose was assailed by the smells peculiar to the village. Although he did not know it at once the main smells were compounded of dried fish, onions, ginger and tea.

Children of both sexes foregathered first in front of them. There was perhaps a minute of doubt and indecision in the bright young Oriental faces, and then the appearance of Ahmed and Yusuf set them dancing and pointing. Older people came, full of curiosity, bunching in the background and marvelling at the size of the British party which their countrymen had brought along.

Britwell studied them, using his senses to the full. All the men were clean-shaven, except the very old, who had long wispy beards from the very tips of their chins. Many of them had slightly unhealthy looking scarlet lips, stained by their habit of chewing the betel nut. They were dressed in a calf-length cotton garment which was draped around them like a Malayan *sarong*. The colours were many and varied.

In seconds, the Boli brothers had gone through the curious villagers. The crowd thickened in depth while the journalist studied the banana and papaya trees, noted the white flowers of the palms and marvelled at the great greenish-black mangoes which gave the settlement much of its atmosphere.

The women were demure, but frankly curious as they peered over men's shoulders. The older ones were finely wrinkled about the cheekbones, the mouths and the eyes. One or two of the younger ones wore white flowers in their hair. This caused a thaw among the soldiers, and many a man grinned in anticipation of having a native girl friend.

There was a stir among the crowd. A gap opened up and three men came through. The first was a short man of mature years, with a bald head and a long thin grey beard. Grinning broadly at his shoulder was a younger, familiar face: that of the boy, Shan.

Shan's reappearance caused a surprise among the newcomers, but it was short-lived because the third man, who towered above the other two, was wearing a Japanese jockey cap such as Britwell had adopted.

Instinctively, the British shifted their positions and gripped their weapons. Shan and the old man hesitated, while the crowd closed in around the third man, masking him from the guns of the newcomers. The atmosphere was tense for a few seconds before the third man laughed.

He had a long Roman nose and a pointed chin. His grin showed a flash of gold fillings. 'Don't worry about the Jap tifter, boys. I'm Archie Rondell. I head an independent unit of the Special Service

Detachment. Welcome to Daung Bazar. We've been expecting you.'

Britwell, with a flash of inspiration, guessed that this incongruous figure was none other than 'John Peel.'

14

Major Archibald Rondell assured McCool, Britwell and all the others that their approach had been noted by village scouts some fifteen minutes earlier. They had been allowed to advance unimpeded because the Bolis had been recognized at the outset.

On all sides, the Burmese fell back, making a clearing in front of the most imposing stilted houses, which were known as *bashas*. Very briefly, the British introduced themselves to each other. Rondell was then quick to present Britwell, McCool and Corporal Judd to the headman of the village, who was at his side.

'Mashraf, I have the honour to introduce to you Mr Harry Britwell, a British journalist. Also Sergeant McCool and Corporal Judd of a commando outfit. Gentlemen, meet our good friend, Mashraf, who is your host.'

The commandos shuffled, coughed and nodded, smiling broadly. When Britwell made a move to shake hands, the old Burmese took both his hands in his own and politely bowed over them.

'Sahib, I am honoured to know you. Welcome to our humble village. You already know my grandson, Shan and the brothers Boli, who, I hope have been of some service to you.'

'Thank you, Mashraf, for the first words of welcome since we dropped rather awkwardly from the skies. We are glad to be in your midst, and without the help of your grandson and his friends we should still be out in the great wilderness dodging the enemies of our country.'

Britwell glanced around for Shan, but the boy had gone into the background somewhere, hiding no doubt until the matter of his stealing the quinine had been aired. Mashraf clapped his hands for service, while Rondell looked over the new arrivals and hurriedly assessed their general health and fitness for active strikes against the enemy.

'You must have been annoyed when

Shan stole the quinine,' he murmured apologetically, 'but I was running a fever. He knew I needed it in a hurry and Daung Bazar is rapidly becoming an area of strategic importance.'

Mashraf cleared his throat and ran his long fingers through the straggle of his beard. 'Put down your weapons, gentlemen. You are in no danger here. You will all feel better when you have had a few glasses of rice wine.'

The commandos hesitated at first, but when McCool lowered his weapon to the ground they relaxed and squatted in a circle in front of the big *basha*. Britwell found himself between the headman and Rondell sitting cross-legged.

For the two NCO's and himself there were glass tumblers. Lightly clad young women in cotton costumes of various bright colours handed them out, along with clay bowls for the others. Two girls then started to move around the circle pouring tepid wine from clay containers.

Several thirsty men had already sipped the concoction by the time all were served.

'To your health and that of your King,' Mashraf suggested, in his slow English.

Glasses and bowls were raised and all drank. The first drink went down quickly. Tongues were loosened. Words of appreciation slipped easily from the lips of the thirsty men in the accent of Liverpool. The drinking vessels were speedily refilled. Men ogled the girls with the vessels. The young women's faces were animated and friendly in a cautious sort of way.

Rondell watched the effects of the wine on the soldiers. He grinned sardonically. He inclined his head in the direction of Britwell.

'You will have much to write about in the next few days, if all goes well.'

'Do you have any means for sending out my work?'

'Nothing speedy, but I can guarantee that it will get through in time. Unfortunately, my radio failed some little time ago. I don't suppose you have one with you?'

'Yes, I believe we can supply you with one, major. It's been through some pretty hectic times, but I fancy it still works.'

'Capital! Capital! Now I shall be able to get my advance information about local conditions back to base and receive new orders. As you know, HQ is quite keen to locate an airstrip in this region. We need one without delay. The Japs have a supply dump not far from here and it is likely to be greatly increased as they are pushing a railway line towards us from the south.'

'How long have you been here, major?' Britwell asked, his curiosity mounting.

'Oh, more or less from the beginning. I was in the rice exporting business in peacetime. I retired to join the army for a short spell and then came back again. Excuse me.'

Rondell turned to the headman and exchanged a few short sharp sentences in the local Burmese dialect. Britwell took the opportunity to study the major more closely. The major had gone native in the matter of dress. Outlining his muscular chest was a white cotton vest. Lower down he wore the traditional Burmese skirt-like attire. Later, Britwell was to find out that it was called a *lungyi*. Rondell's was bright red, perhaps a likely colour for a man whose code name was John Peel. Underneath the *lungyi*, he had his army revolver belted to his waist.

The conversation in Burmese came to an end. 'Sergeant, I'd like you to make sure that all your men overlook Shan's misdemeanour in running off with the quinine. A lot depends upon it. He acted in my best interests.'

McCool nodded without saying anything.

Rondell resumed. 'Shan will appear in a minute. I want you and your men to leave your weapons here and follow him to the village's bathing place. Bathe where he tells you and be back in a half hour. A proper meal will be waiting for you by then.

'Try and relax, but don't let your men get too boisterous. That rice wine is potent. It could raise difficulties on an empty stomach.'

Already, the men who had heard were rising to their feet and chaffing one another about the prospect of a refreshing bathe, but McCool was not quite ready. He indicated where the radio was, inside the circle.

'I take it we'll be under your command indefinitely, major?'

'That's the general idea, sergeant. The fortunes of war cut you off from your outfit. Now, I've got to make use of you in what could be a deteriorating situation. You've no objections, I hope?'

McCool pushed forward his formidable jaw. 'No, sir. So long as you don't employ us as messenger boys. We *are* supposed to be commandos, 'ighly trained in bush warfare.'

There was a suggestion of venom in Rondell's voice as he replied: 'Rest assured, sergeant, I won't underestimate you in any way. You'll be put in the picture directly after your meal.'

Rondell then assumed a stance of absolute military correctness. It was as though the 'attention' position oozed out of his personality rather than any sudden move. McCool blinked and remembered his drill and the hours and hours of square-bashing in his days as a private.

He drew himself up and saluted. Rondell returned the salute, in spite of his Japanese headgear.

'Carry on, sergeant.'

McCool broke off and hurried after his men, who were being led away by Shan. Britwell wondered how they would hit it off, this long-term jungle dwelling officer and the short-tempered NCO from Liverpool.

A small brown boy who could not have been more than four years of age danced around the ring where the commandos had been seated. His bare feet were in and out of the weapons and packs left there, but none were touched. He halted between the two men and pushed a couple of brown-leafed cigars into Rondell's hand. He was thanked in the local dialect.

'Fancy a smoke, Britwell? Try one of these. A real Burma cheroot. And a Japanese match!'

The glint of mischief had been in the major's eyes before the cheroots had been delivered. Britwell could not be sure why it was there. Either the major was looking forward to a clash of wills with Dick McCool, or it had just struck him how incongruous Britwell and he looked. Two mature Englishmen, both in their late thirties and doing their wartime bit for the old country in the borrowed headgear issued to conscripts of Imperial Nippon for use in jungle conditions.

Scoop turned up the peak of his cap and tentatively put a cheroot between his lips. The Japanese match stick flared into flame. The journalist sucked and was pleased that the smoke inhaled did not appear to be too heavy.

He grinned appreciatively. 'I wonder if the chaps who supplied us with these caps went to the same military tailor?'

'Now there's a theory,' Rondell replied, with mock interest. 'Tell you what, though, my man didn't have a lot of character. He was found to be slothful in military business.'

* * *

In all, Britwell spent a mere ten minutes at the bathing place. He was anxious to further acquaintance with Major Rondell and the headman, Mashraf. Inwardly, he was cross with himself for having infringed upon his non-combatant status. Although his first fall from virtue had been the occasion when he fought for his life in single combat, he was angry at the way circumstances had forced him to take up arms again.

He felt that in the eyes of those who knew him, he could no longer wear his war correspondent's flashes. The Japs, apparently, did not want to know about such niceties and there was no point in further deluding himself or others. Consequently, when he joined the small select group in front of Mashraf's *basha* for the meal, he had removed his shoulder flashes and hidden them away.

Mashraf and Rondell were in the small eating circle, along with McCool, Judd and a muscular, stocky Burmese stranger of about thirty years. The unexpected appearance of this fellow in the general group had the effect of postponing discussions of a military nature about the future. Mashraf hastened to introduce the stranger, who had his head shaved, but wore a thin moustache. His clothing consisted of a green vest and a blue *lungyi*. He toyed with a metal disc hung about his neck on a chain.

'Gentlemen, may I introduce to you a man of my village, Chit Khalique. He is a captain in the Burmese Rifles at present on leave from his regiment. The badge he wears is that of the peacock.'

Chit rose to his feet on slightly bowed legs and courteously shook hands with all present except the headman. Clearly, Chit had not long since returned to the village. His anxiety to exchange information with Mashraf made him break out in his own language while the food was being served.

Britwell, McCool and Judd felt cut off, but Rondell fed them with scraps of translation, assuring them that Chit was only bringing himself up to date because he had been away for three years.

Again, women appeared to serve the men. The main course was of curried fish and rice. Fruit followed. Bananas, cocoa-nuts and other exotic varieties. After that, for those who wanted it there was tea in large quantities, and an abundance of rice wine.

Presently, the two other groups forgot their inhibitions and sprawled about, lazing, smoking and talking about this and that, and assessing their mixed fortunes since the crash landing. Having ascertained that all his 'table' guests had finished eating, Mashraf clapped his hands, issued instructions to four men who appeared and handed round cigars.

While the routine of lighting them was going on, a three foot bamboo fence was rigged around the small select circle to give them greater privacy. Conversation could have been heard over the top of it but the villagers and the commandos discreetly kept away.

Rondell coughed to clear his throat. 'The time has come, gents, to hold a council of war. Firstly, the radio worked well. I was able to send out a report to my base in Imphal and to receive instructions about making use of your commando outfit for imminent operations in this area.

'Although you were never intended to

function under my command, you could not have come at a more opportune time. This far, most of my activities have been limited to scouting and intelligence work. Now, with your co-operation, I shall be able to go over to the offensive.'

He unrolled a large sheet of white paper and spread it out in front of Britwell and the two NCO's.

'This is a rough map of our area. You can see the north-south road, which you crossed to get here, and the location of this village. East and south-east of us there is a high ridge with two prominent vantage points on it.

'The nearer of the two pinnacles has a pagoda on the top of it. It is known locally as the Place of the Chins, and at the moment is under our control. Not so the other small peak. That is located further south. The Japs are using it as a strong point, and the locals refer to it as Nippon Hill.'

He indicated the saddle-like pass half way between the pagoda and the enemy strong point which afforded a means of getting through from the tracked valley further east to the impressive north-south road a mile or so to westward.

His spatulate forefinger then moved across the map from the saddle to the wooded slopes below Nippon Hill on the west side.

'This area is of growing significance. The railway track being constructed almost parallel with the road is almost as far north as Nippon Hill and the gradient west of it. In these trees at this moment is a Jap supply dump of quite useful proportions.

'Every day, the track is being pushed further north. The builders of it are mostly captured prisoners. British, Indians and Chinese. I need hardly tell you that railway-borne supplies are likely to increase the size of the dump to vast proportions.

'Furthermore, Allied High Command are hoping to locate a new airstrip a few miles west of that railhead, the dump and Nippon Hill. So, you can see how we're fixed.'

McCool, almost out of character, was grinning with the prospects of drastic action, while Judd coughed on his cheroot and had to have his back slapped.

Rondell glanced around the ring and tried to assess the effect of his words. Before McCool could reply, the major spoke again. 'I shall not be leading you on this caper. My fever attack has left me weak — '

'No need to worry, major,' the sergeant blurted out, 'me and the boys can 'it the track, down country a piece, maybe the locomotive itself. Then we can blow the dump sky 'igh at our leisure!'

'Your zeal is commendable, sergeant,' Rondell conceded, 'but I have to point out that the railhead is well guarded. So is the dump. And munitions of war are very valuable. My aim is to thin out the dump by stealth and rehouse the munitions elsewhere, perhaps in the pagoda.'

McCool was stunned into temporary silence.

'I agree with the major,' Britwell put in mildly, 'as to the value of the Jap stores. In stealing from the dump we should be extracting the enemy's teeth.'

The rather high-pitched voice of

Captain Chit was next heard.

'Perhaps a diversionary raid on the railhead would help. I wonder if the guards at the dump could be drawn away?'

'That's the sort of scheme I could approve,' Rondell put in brusquely. 'Captain Chit will lead the diversion, and I'm sure you'll all do well, provided you don't overdo things.'

McCool looked dismayed and deliberately turned away from the Burmese officer. In order to allay the tension building in the group, Britwell asked a question.

'If I can be of any use, count me in. I don't intend to sit on my backside in the market-place while all this is going on.'

'I've thought of that,' Rondell admitted. 'We can use you with the locals who will actually perform the sneak raid. I'll set up the operation for tomorrow. You chaps deserve one sound night's sleep before going into action.'

The major stood up, nodded to the headman, adjusted his *lungyi* and indicated that the council of war was over.

15

Long before sundown, Rondell called a medical parade. Boils were dressed. Prickly heat was treated. A repellent was used to ward off the mosquitoes, and every man's bruises, cuts and strains were attended to in some way or another.

One line of the stilted *bashas* were totally evacuated in favour of the fighting troops, so that they could get one restful night's sleep before going over to the offensive. Mostly, the troops used the upper rooms, the walls of which withstood some of the cool breezes and the nightly drop in temperature.

Rondell had his own squad of lookouts, who kept watch all night around the periphery of the village. The families who gave up their *bashas* retired into lesser structures which were not stilted. There was no grumbling. Daung Bazar was pro-British from the oldest to the youngest.

Every man was given a drink of rice wine as he turned in and advised to forget the war until daybreak. Britwell spent the last half hour of daylight scribbling down vivid impressions of the village on his pad. Rondell was already asleep in the other half of the upper room and Chit was sound asleep on the ground below, between the stilts.

As the light faded and the cold crept in, the last human noises which the journalist heard came from a *basha* opposite. Two men were quietly singing a ditty peculiar to Liverpool. Presently, their voices faded, and one of their mates asked a question in a slurred voice.

'Lofty, will you tell me one thing before you start snorin'? What 'appened to the war? It seems to 'ave given Daung Bazar the go-by.'

Britwell felt that the air was full of speculation, but no one attempted to answer the pertinent query and quite soon after that the sound of snoring carried across the clearing.

★ ★ ★

The hens and other livestock started the day, and soon the commandos were out and about, sniffing around the breakfast fires and wondering what the day had in store for them. The food consisted of eggs and fruit, washed down with tea.

Major Rondell stepped between the groups while some men were still drinking and smoking. He informed McCool that he would do a weapon inspection in ten minutes. The sergeant urged his men through their last preparations and lined them up in two rows, facing south.

Rondell acknowledged his salute and at once had them stood at ease. His inspection was rather informal. Some who might have resented his taking over control soon realized that all he was interested in was the efficiency of the men and their weapons. He then introduced Captain Chit and advised them that they would be setting out very shortly.

Britwell moved among the restless fighting men, exchanging banter and chaff with as many as he could. When they were called to attention, he was standing between Mick Judd and Everton chatting about chin stubble and the changes it made in a man's appearance. Everton already had a black beard, and he started to fancy himself with it.

Chit had things to say. 'Clear of the village, you must keep close together. The mist will be thick for a while. There will be very little time for rest before we reach the railhead. Another thing. If we run into Japs, we fight, but we try not to give away our presence to other parties, otherwise our route to the railway might be blocked.'

Britwell stood with his arms folded, watching them go by in single file. Most of them grinned at him, and one or two gave him Churchill's 'V for Victory' sign. Flanking him one on either side were Rondell and Mashraf, and standing behind them were Shan and the brothers Boli.

When the last man had moved out of sight, Britwell turned to the major with a broad grin on his face. 'And now, what follows?'

'You go native, amigo.'

Rondell was grinning: so were the three young Burmese at the rear. Shan produced a bright yellow *lungyi* and a cream vest.

'These are for you,' the major informed him. 'You must shave first. Young Burmans as a rule don't wear facial hair. We have hot water for you, and you can borrow my shaving kit. Shan will show you how to wear the *lungyi*. I've got some interviewing to do and a message to send.'

So saying, 'John Peel' nodded, grinned and strolled off to the hut where the radio had been housed. Two or three natives who had walked in from other locations through the night, rose from the ground to give him their information.

Shan brought the bowl of water and the shaving tackle. 'It is good for us to be united again, Sahib Britwell, and to know that you have been selected to go on missions with Ahmed, Yusuf and me. They have told me many things about your fighting qualities since I left the soldiers in such a hurry.'

Britwell stopped lathering his face and

grinned ruefully. 'You must understand, Shan, I'm not supposed to be a fighting soldier, at all. I came into this country of yours to observe and write about what was going on. If my superiors knew how I'd been behaving since I got here I'd be in serious trouble.'

Shan pushed back his coolie hat and scratched his short-cropped black hair. He wrinkled his forehead and blinked his brown eyes in the frankest of expressions.

'If that is so, Sahib Britwell, your superiors don't know the conditions here. The Japanese and the jungle will not let a stranger be neutral — if that is the correct word. A man, *any* man, has to fight to survive.'

Shan chattered on, while Britwell finished his shave and was shown how to drape the yellow *lungyi* round his loins and fix it safely at the waist. The cream vest was a little on the tight side across his chest, but there was plenty of stretch in it.

'Do I keep the jockey cap?'

'Yes, sahib, but if we run into Japs you must hide it quickly. Major Rondell has left you a revolver and a belt. If you want to wear them I think you will have to strip off the *lungyi* again and put them next to your skin.'

This, Britwell patiently agreed to do. Yusuf offered him a *dah*, but he refused it, retaining the shorter knife which he had used before. He grumbled that his arms, shoulders and legs were too pale for him to pass as a native, but they assured him that the sun would soon tan him.

He had discarded his boots and was trying on gym shoes as a substitute when Rondell stuck his head out of the radio hut and shouted something in Burmese which made the Bolis and Shan anxious to start out. Having been thoroughly inspected himself, Britwell studied the others. Shan was wearing the same sort of white baggy trousers and smock as when they had first met. The Bolis had changed their apparel overnight. Now, they were wearing faded pale green *lungyis* and lightweight turbans of the same colour.

'We must go now, sahib, if you are ready?'

Shan, who had picked up a water container made out of the skin of a small animal, glanced up at him inquiringly. Britwell professed himself ready. Ahmed tapped the tool sharpening stone with the blade of his *dah* as they moved off. Mashraf appeared and saluted them with a clasped handshake, while Rondell's head, resplendent with earphones, briefly appeared to call a farewell.

Britwell felt drawn to glance this way and that as they moved through the lesser thoroughfares of the village and attracted the attention of the villagers. He caught and held the attention of two or three girls with white flowers in their hair before he went through the protective stockade on the heels of Shan.

* * *

Ninety minutes later, Yusuf headed them up the last of the slope which led to the isolated and age-old pagoda known to visitors as the Place of the Chins.

The Burmese had husbanded Britwell's strength and picked reasonable going, mindful of the unaccustomed *lungyi* and the rubber shoes. At first, the mist had bothered him, but after a time it cleared and he had stepped out boldly, keeping up with their accustomed pace through the jungle paths and wooded slopes.

The last of the trees and shrubs thinned out and the pagoda was outlined right above them, guarded at each corner by a stone figure which to Britwell resembled a wolf in gold trappings. His breath was labouring, but he had to ask questions.

'What is the significance of the four stone animals, Shan?'

For once, the Burmese youth was slow to answer. His attention was elsewhere, now that they were in the open. The Bolis were scowling as if they had sensed the presence of the enemy. In the nearside wall of the ancient temple was an opening, and through it, half-hidden in shadow was a shoulder and part of the head of a huge reclining figure of Buddha.

'You must ask my sister, some time. She talks well and she has more time than I have.'

Shan's answer came from considerably

further away than Britwell had expected. He found when he looked around that his companions had satisfied themselves that none of the enemy were anywhere concealed on the approach slopes. Now they were behaving as if the pagoda itself might be the hiding place of enemies.

Ahmed moved off to one side and Yusuf to the other. Shan studied the stone guardians of the temple from one knee. Britwell studied them each in turn. He perceived that there was some sort of superstition affecting them, and he undertook to go on ahead, a course which was approved.

In the last thirty yards, when his comrades had dropped further behind, his heart thumped. What if there *were* Japs waiting for them? He perceived his comrades crawling forward in the short grass, moving like newts, trailing their *dahs* instead of tails. He found their caution admirable, but disquieting. Loosening his borrowed revolver, he gathered himself and raced for the nearest of the four great Chin Tae figures.

His lungs were bursting almost as he

crouched behind its towering twelve foot bulk, still studying the entrance. The customary jungle noises were behind him now. The critical moment was near.

Acting upon impulse, he laid down the revolver and hurriedly pulled off his gym shoes which were drawing his feet. Gripping them both in one hand, he hurled them into the entrance and grabbed the firearm.

Several seconds dragged by. Suddenly a small furry creature came out of the opening, moving so fast that it was only a blur to the naked eye. Nothing else happened. Cautiously, he straightened up and walked to the gaping entrance.

The place was unoccupied. In taking off his foot gear he had complied with a basic Burmese custom. This act, done without thought, further endeared him to the three locals who then came up swiftly and confirmed that no enemy personnel was in the vicinity.

16

A few minutes before eleven o'clock that morning, Captain Chit and the commandos were resting up in the last of the tree cover on a slope some seventy yards above and to the east of the end of the Japanese railway line.

The party was tensed up for action after their protracted trek from Daung Bazar.

A locomotive had chugged in from the south five minutes earlier. The prisoner labourers, a motley ill-fed collection of British soldiers, Indians and Burmese had been given a long overdue work break and they were gathered together taking what shelter they could between two great heaps of wooden sleepers on the near side of the track end.

The Japanese guards were numerous, but they had drawn away from their charges to greet a score or so of fresh troops who had just arrived on the train, which consisted of two goods wagons and two passenger carriages.

Beyond the sleeper piles and the end of steel were two Japanese lorries which had earlier come down from the north.

On higher ground, to the east of the would-be ambushers, was the widespread area of teak and bamboo which had become the dumping ground for Japanese military stores of all descriptions. At a much greater height and distance, above the dump to the east, was the southern-most pinnacle of the vast ridge which had been nicknamed by the locals Nippon Hill.

From the rear of a clump of *bizat* bushes, Chit had pointed out all the points of military significance. He had missed nothing, but his exhaustive survey of the whole position had left the commandos more nervous than when they first arrived and considerably short on patience. There were grumblings about time being wasted.

Judd licked his lips and nudged McCool with an elbow. 'Sarge, I think the boys are right. We ought to 'ave attacked when the Nip guards pulled out to welcome the new arrivals. Every minute lost is goin' to make our task that much 'arder.'

McCool gripped his Sten with all his strength. 'All right, all right, Mick, I'll tell 'im!'

All through the trek Chit had shown his expert knowledge of jungle craft. In holding back the Burmese officer might have some other item in reserve. So McCool had thought. But as the seconds ticked by, he, too, thought an error of judgement was being made.

'Captain Chit, I agree with all my boys. We're wastin' time. The moment when our strike could 'ave 'ad its biggest impact 'as already gone. What are we waitin' for?'

Chit favoured him with a small, tight grin. 'Before I left the village, the major said not to attack before eleven. He was using the radio. Maybe there was something in his mind, something which could help us when we do attack.'

The nervous sergeant moved away from his short, stocky local superior and maintained a poker expression while his men looked to him for a positive lead. He looked to be seething with suppressed anger.

The chatter of the excited Japanese, the steam coming from the loco and the noise made by a mechanic tuning up an engine for a time drowned the new sounds which came from the sky. Everton, as usual, was the first to detect them. As soon as he heard them, he turned to Chit, who stuck up a thumb and grinned broadly.

'Aircraft! That's what the major had in mind!'

The airborne sounds were coming from the north. This caused every man to turn in that direction and peer up through the tree foliage in an effort to catch a glimpse of them.

McCool, who was still on edge, called: 'Well, Everton, are they ours or theirs?'

'Ours, I'd say, sarge. If you wanted me to guess I'd say Beaufighters. But you'll know in a minute.'

'Give them the time to make their first strike, then we will hit them!' Chit's high-pitched voice now sounded as excited as that of any of the others.

Rifles, grenades and Stens were easily to hand as a trio of diving planes lined up on the road, and then upon the railroad track beside it. Before they arrived, Chit was on his feet. Even though the rest had been ready for a long time, he took them by surprise when he flitted from tree to tree, gradually moving lower down the slope and into the open.

The relaxed Japanese were slow to scatter. Down came the first plane, its guns roaring in sudden menace. Small shells ripped up the loose soil on the east side of the track and accounted for about half a dozen enemy personnel.

The second did not come down for nearly ten seconds and that gave the guards and some of the fresh troops a chance to look around and scatter. Upwards of a dozen came racing for the trees where the British ambushers were lurking.

McCool's Sten started the head-on destruction of men running for cover. Four crumpled in as many seconds, while the second British plane, its weapons aimed more accurately than the first, poured its stream of projectiles into the cab of the loco, and sliced through the roofs of the wagons and carriages. Human cries of agony were drowned in the oppressive uproar of the diving planes.

Captain Chit, a flying grotesque figure in his green vest and blue *lungyi* raced past the two heaps of sleepers, oblivious to the danger. His attention was on the two trucks parked on the far side of the track. He slithered to a halt, thirty yards away, set his feet apart and gave attention to his grenades.

A hefty lob sent the first one over the top of the nearer stationary vehicle. It landed on the second's top, exploded one second later and accounted for the mechanic and another soldier who were hiding in the cab. As the lorry blew apart, the little Burmese ducked low, became aware of soldiers hiding under the nearer lorry, and wondered if they had enough guts to retaliate.

As the third diving fighter duplicated the damage done by the second, he rolled his other grenade under the first lorry and awaited the explosion. A man who hurriedly tried to crawl clear was shot in the head with a revolver bullet.

And then Chit was retreating towards the trees, aware that all three planes had done their first run. They would be back, and firing again into the misused mass of enemy equipment shrouded in smoke. Up went the second lorry in an orange sheet of flame.

Japs looking for a target were further distracted as the small Burmese raced for the trees with his *lungyi* held above knee level. He hastened into the trees, quite breathless, just as the three Beaufighters turned again and screamed down into their second marauding run. McCool, smiling crookedly, grabbed him by the shoulder as he moved nearer the latter's tree cover.

'We knocked off about eleven Nips who came straight at us, captain,' he yelled hoarsely. 'You did well with the trucks.'

Again came the staccato rattle of shells. Chit had to shout to make himself heard. 'I'm glad your men were so effective. Now, we go.' He pointed up the slope, wide of the dump.

McCool, as usual, was dissatisfied. 'What about them prisoners? You must 'ave seen 'em when you went round the other side. We ought to be able to spring the lot of 'em, with a bit of luck!'

Chit stood firm by his decision. 'No, it is beyond the bounds of this operation. They are weak through lack of good food. They couldn't keep up with us. Their chance will come another day!'

Everton appeared alongside of them. 'One of the carriages is burnin', sarge. Not much left of their rollin' stock!'

'Yes, yes,' Chit answered hurriedly. 'Good, good. Now we must go. Up that way. We must draw some of their men away from the dump!'

By sharp gestures, the Burmese officer indicated to the others what he had in mind. McCool, flanked by Everton, stood firm for a time, but most of his men, unaware of his disagreement, shouldered their weapons and moved after the local man in sprightly fashion.

As the planes pulled out, climbed for altitude and headed back to base,

McCool shook his Sten in frustration and reluctantly went after the others.

Twenty minutes later, Chit raised his arm and indicated a halt. The commandos were soon around him, breathless through their retreat up the slope. They squatted on the ground and followed his pointing finger towards the fringe of trees which marked the north perimeter of the Japanese dumping ground.

At first they saw nothing. Everton persisted, and soon he was able to make out some sort of a defensive position blocked in by a pile of railway sleepers. McCool reluctantly awaited instructions.

Sam Blade, the last to close up, pointed back in the direction of the rail track. 'There's about twenty Nips on our back trail! An' they look as if they mean business.'

'Good, everything is going to plan. Sergeant, I'd like your best grenade thrower to lob one over that barricade. That will disturb the guards an' bring some of them away after us. Now, who will do the throwing?'

Several men read McCool's thoughts,

but Chit had truly won the respect of his British followers. After some slight hesitation, three men volunteered for the job. McCool nominated Lofty Littleton, a man whose cricket had almost taken him into the country eleven before the war broke out.

Lofty uncoiled himself like a baseball pitcher, and his comrades watched with interest as the 'pineapple' sailed through the air towards the target. It fell a yard or two short, but its blast had the effect of knocking the sleepers onto the men taking shelter behind it. There were casualties.

Chit briefly studied the position lower down the slope, and confidently waved the marauders forward again. His route was still uphill, approximately towards Nippon Hill. McCool was surprised, but he did not query the decision.

★　★　★

Meanwhile, Britwell and his three comrades were half way along the length of the ridge, at the lowest point of the saddle between the two high points. They had witnessed the strike at the railhead through a pair of binoculars, which had been secreted away inside the pagoda.

From time to time, they had spotted the commandos withdrawing up the slope. The grenade thrown into the dump had brought them up to date with their observations. The quartette came together behind a low clump of bamboos and took stock of the whole situation.

Shan had high hopes of slipping into the dump along its northern edge and lifting a few useful items, but Ahmed's study of the fortified Nippon Hill changed things. From among the camouflaged field guns, fox holes and machine-gun nests, a new force of Japanese were emerging.

Grudgingly, Britwell surrendered the glasses. Shan, who had taken them, counted the Japs he could see emerging from the stronghold.

'About a dozen men. Chit and the commandos could be caught unawares between the two groups, if they don't turn towards the north quite soon.'

'Chit will see them, but not yet for a

while,' Yusuf opined.

Ahmed added: 'We must abandon our idea of entering the dump and do what we can to prevent our friends from being surrounded.'

'How shall we do it?' Britwell asked practically.

'First we lose altitude,' Shan answered matter of factly. 'When we are between the men from the Hill and our forces, we shall strike. In doing our strike we shall warn Chit, and he will do the rest.'

Already, the four were moving swiftly downhill, most of their attention on the going underfoot. The saddle was sparsely furnished with trees and bushes, but soon they were in cover and some of the strain went out of their movements.

Britwell was troubled. His mood communicated itself to the others.

'What is it, sahib?' Ahmed inquired patiently.

'Our task will be difficult with just a service revolver and a few *dahs*. Don't you agree?'

Ahmed shrugged his muscular shoulders. His brother grinned, and Shan seemed to be taking the matter lightly. He remarked: 'We must take over some of their weapons. That will even things up.'

'Don't forget the darts,' Yusuf murmured.

Britwell looked puzzled. He had not seen the Boli brothers collect a pair of bamboo tubes and a handful of poisoned darts from the cache within the pagoda. Clearly, his education was to be filled out a little more in the near future.

A half hour later, they pulled up behind yet another clump of bamboo. A brief, spirited conversation took place between the three natives. From time to time, their glances took in Britwell, who hoped they had something purposeful for him to do.

'So what is my part in the coming encounter, friends?' he enquired patiently.

'We want you to separate from us and distract the men coming from the Hill with your revolver, sahib,' Shan explained.

'While you make a sneak flank attack on them?'

All three nodded and smiled broadly like mischievous children. He agreed, and was filled in as to the exact position of the platoon coming down from the Hill. Their assessment of the situation was true to within a minute.

As the first four Japs moved cautiously down the slope, moving from bole to bole, fifty yards wide of him, Britwell stepped clear of his teak tree, rested the revolver on his left forearm and squeezed the trigger.

It was a fair distance for that type of weapon, and he certainly startled more of the enemy than he hit, but one man who staggered made him confident that he had claimed a victim. As was expected, the infantrymen heading down the slope soon recovered from their fright and turned their attention towards him.

His heart thumped as they closed the gap between them, moving up a yard or two at a time, and seeking to pin down his actual location. Too many men were getting far too close when he first had evidence that his friends were in action. His eyes were busy when a Jap infantryman toppled sideways out of cover and slumped to the ground.

A troubled murmur from his fellows

slowed the advance, but presently another one gave up, having been hit in the shoulder by a dart. A short while later, one of the nearest men broke cover and started forward in a suicidal run, clutching a machine-gun in his arms. Some ten yards away when he was slowing and preparing to spring for cover the blade of a *dah* ripped into his rib cage and dropped him on the spot with no more than a short agonized cry.

Shan's flying figure hurtled through the trees and dropped behind the fallen man, scooping up his automatic weapon. Two rifle shots from different locations were fired at Shan, but they did him no harm. The Burmese boy bided his time, and then dragged the corpse in front of him until he was behind a tree.

For a few tense minutes, all the fighting seemed to have ceased. Britwell could not be sure if there were three or four men in advanced positions. The slight shifting of foliage, the mottled sunlight filtering through the treetops was playing tricks on his eyes. He felt that if he blasted off too sharply he might hit one of his friends.

Consequently, he kept quiet, hoping for some sort of clue as to what they were doing.

Further up the slope a gibbon scolded with monotonous persistency. The rear guard, if it could be called that, began to advance with extreme caution. Another two darts found targets. That thinned them out. They began to get nervous. Nervousness cost them their overall alertness, and soon they were near the dart operators without knowing it.

Another man died before the Burmese' tactics altered. Unknown to Britwell, they had fired all the darts. But, as they had suggested earlier, there were other ways of eliminating the enemy. Ahmed, hidden on the opposite side of the tree bole to an advancing soldier, moved around and dropped his looped turban over the man's head.

The cloth tightened around the unfortunate man's throat. The well-developed wrestler's arm and shoulder muscles did the rest. When the body went limp, Ahmed used the arm of the corpse to wave forward others. He shot two men with a borrowed rifle, and a third would have obeyed the summons had not Yusuf accounted for him by strangulation. Yusuf's victim had grenades. The younger Boli called a piercing cry of warning before lobbing the first of two pineapples into the rear of the first Jap group.

Two more men rose and fell as the explosive cone blew outwards and upwards, blowing a clear hole through the tree-top foliage and letting in the sunlight. The dreadful devastation of the grenades was a signal for the Japs to break cover and run.

Three flying figures in the drab green were soon picked off by the revolver, two rifles and a woodpecker. The echo of shots seemed to rise and fall interminably as the action faded, and birds in their hundreds cleared the trees and hastily winged their way to quieter, safer territory.

There was no time to gloat over their gains. In fact, the Burmese were too well trained for that. Yusuf ran off down the slope to make contact with the other British party. He encountered them within five minutes, and turned north with them.

A simulated bird cry from one Boli to the other had the effect of drawing Ahmed, Shan and Britwell also towards the north. Yusuf returned to them running easily. All was well with the other party, although half a dozen determined Jap troopers had turned north below them.

Britwell's party cautiously walked a converging course with the Japs from the railway. As soon as they were spotted, large and small rocks were sent off down the slope to discourage them. For extra measure, grenades collected from the vanquished party were also rolled down the slope.

A series of damaging explosions decimated and deterred them, so that the survivors prudently called off the exercise and allowed the two victorious allied groups to converge and fall back upon their base.

17

There was a great deal of hand shaking and shoulder thumping as one victorious group fused with the other. Shan and Britwell exchanged details with Captain Chit and McCool as the party continued northward in ones and twos.

Around two o'clock in the afternoon, when they were still a good distance from the village, Chit headed them into a small camp fashioned in a hollow behind a horseshoe outcrop of rock which faced down the slope towards the west.

Rondell was standing in the middle of it, his hands on his hips and a sun helmet on his head, in violent contrast with his vest, *lungyi* and sandals. The broadest of grins bisected his face and brought his Roman nose out like a parrot's beak above his pointed chin.

The Bolis and Shan hurried forward as half a dozen young women left their cooking fires and came to meet them. He figured that they were all in their late teens or early twenties, mature and available for marriage, as the white flowers in their hair suggested.

Their skins were almost copper-coloured. Their cheekbones were high, their eyes dark and bright. Without exception they were slim, elegant and beautifully contoured in their brightly coloured *lungyis* and slack-waisted contrasting blouses.

While the Burmese men and women greeted each other, the perspiring commandos spread out in an admiring crescent, showing a becoming bashfulness quite foreign to their earlier aggressiveness in the ambush.

Rondell called: 'Welcome to our temporary bivouac, men. Take the weight off your feet and prepare to eat. You can see we had confidence in you. The meal has been ready for half an hour.'

The more hungry of the outfit acknowledged the major's words, but others just stood or squatted around, gradually adjusting to the new situation.

Britwell was entranced with the coming together of Shan and a beautiful lissom creature with a delicate heart-shaped face who matched him for size. The girl and boy threw their arms about each other in a warm embrace which fed the soldiers' hunger for women.

The girl wore a bottle-green *lungyi* and a paler green cotton blouse swelled in front by her small firm breasts. The blouse pouted above the navel and accentuated her extreme slimness.

As the soldiers started to settle down and murmur about the surprise meeting, the Burmese terminated their greetings and looked around them sheepishly. Shan's eyes happened to fall upon Britwell. The boy took the girl by the hand and led her over to be introduced.

'Britwell, sahib, this is my big sister, Shin. She is happy to make your acquaintance.'

Mildly embarrassed by this signal honour, Britwell whipped off his masking sun spectacles, took her hand in his as she did a brief curtsy and smiled nervously.

'Pleased to meet you, Shin. Your brother has spoken of you to me before.'

He raised the delicate hand to his lips

and kissed it. At that moment it seemed the best possible thing to do.

She murmured: 'It is I who am honoured, sahib. Allow me to fetch you some wine.'

He had visions of old film star favourites such as Dorothy Lamour and Merle Oberon as her mobile lips parted and flashed him a smile which would have done more than justice to an advertisement for brighter teeth. As she withdrew, he studied her upright stance and elegant way of moving.

Britwell murmured: 'Shin is very beautiful, Shan. I am surprised that she is not already married.'

'Others have said this before you, sahib, but remember that many of our menfolk are away fighting in the army.'

The girl returned quickly without unseemly haste. She indicated a flat stone which would serve well as a seat, and when he was seated she handed over a tumbler and filled it for him. After that, she withdrew and busied herself with others who were equally thirsty.

The meal consisted of rice, inevitably,

and meat. No one disclosed the type of meat before the start, but some snake, squirrel and a portion of wild pig had enhanced the stew. Rondell encouraged the British to talk as they ate. Britwell who was equally curious about the clash by the railhead also listened well and asked questions of his own.

From time to time, one or other of the half dozen male villagers who had come along with the provisions and extra ammunition, reported to the major from a lookout position on the camp's perimeter.

The women were as efficient as any trained waitresses in the restaurants of big cities. They cleared away without loss of time and, presently, Rondell's eating circle became instead a smoking and briefing session.

'Men, I'm gratified with the start you've made in actively harassing the enemy. However, we can expect them to counter-attack before very long, and let us not forget that they could soon figure out our village base. These loyal Burmese will be in the firing line when they realize that Daung Bazar is consistently pro-British.

'You'll be in action again tonight.' He paused to let his words sink in. 'I want you to hit that stores base before they find out we're continuing the offensive. Bring away from it, if you can, mines, machine-guns, mortars and the like. Plenty of ammunition. We can always use rifles, pistols and grenades. It's a good thing to fight the enemy with his own tools.'

'Where do we 'ave to carry all this loot to, sir?' McCool asked seriously.

'To the pagoda above the village. With a bit of luck you might find some mules. That will make your task easier. Strike after dark, using stealth. If I hear any big bangs, I'll know you had trouble getting away.'

The discussion moved on. Rondell filled in details and various commandos demanded more information. After some twenty minutes, the major seemed to have satisfied even the most searching questioner. He stood up, stretched his arms and did a couple of knee bends. He was lighting a cheroot when Britwell asked his first question.

'I gather that the whole party stays here and rests, so as to be fit to move off to the south late in the evening. But me, what do *I* do?'

Rondell sucked on his cigar, found it to his liking and nodded.

'As far as the present is concerned, I'd like you to make records of today's operations. The notes will come in handy when you can get your copy away, and it would benefit me to read them myself.

'About tonight. If we haven't been disturbed by the time to mount the new operation, I'd like you to stay right here, along with — say — one fleet-footed Burmese. I shall have my lookouts posted in the saddle, nearer the pagoda, towards Nippon Hill and nearer the dump. If you stayed here, they could bring any urgent information to you and you could decide what to do. I'll be back in the village by that time. What do you think?'

Britwell toyed with his spectacles. 'That would be quite a responsibility. I'll do it though. Who are you planning to leave with me?'

'I'll decide that later, if you don't mind. If all goes well, the returning ambushers will contact you here. Then you can move on with them up to the pagoda. One way and another, we're in for an eventful night.'

Everyone of the original party had heard these latter exchanges. No one argued about the prophecy. Some went off into a deep sleep within minutes. Others graphically described their personal view of the caper down by the end of steel.

Presently, with a not unpleasant touch of writer's cramp, Britwell closed his pad and rested his head on his arm. The last thing he saw before he dozed off was a distant view of the girl, Shin, making something out of split bamboo and liana.

* * *

'John Peel' was the first to slip away.

The commando party, augmented on this occasion by the Bolis and Shan, left the camp about eight o'clock. Britwell toasted their health in rice wine, shook hands with most of them, and relaxed again. He found that he had dozed, and when he revived once more he looked around for his native partner, seeing no one. The trees around the horseshoe grew sufficiently close to put the whole area in shadow, now that the sun had shifted round to westward.

He scrambled to his feet, unhitched his borrowed revolver and began to prowl. Unaccountably, he was nervous. Something prevented his calling out, and when a slim arm came out from behind a tree, holding a coolie hat by the chin band, he started visibly and almost cried out.

'Who is it?' he asked hoarsely.

Shin stepped clear of the tree bole and held the hat towards him.

'You look disappointed, Sahib Britwell. Would you have preferred my brother, or one of the others, as your companion?'

'No, er, no, Shin. I wouldn't have it otherwise. But in leaving you here hasn't the major put you in some danger?'

She smiled as she looked up at him.

For the first time he noticed that she had changed her attire. Baggy black pants and a smock had taken the place of her *lungyi* and blouse, and her ear-length jet black hair was hidden under another coolie hat which was shaped like a symbol.

'We are all in some danger, sahib. You may be surprised to know that I can outrun my brother over a good distance. Here, I made this for you. You do not look handsome in that Japanese soldier's cap. And if you want to change into your khaki when the night grows cooler, I have your other clothes with me.'

'I, well, I don't know what to say. You've thought of everything, Shin.'

She nodded and gave him her most fetching smile. 'We shall be here for a long time. It is important that we get on well together.'

He nodded, reached for her and received the coolie hat into his hand. Discarding the jockey cap, he tried it on and found that it fitted him, although he would have to get used to it.

'It looks good on you, but it is better for fending off the sun. I will show you

261

where your clothes are, if you wish.'

'Please show me, Shin, and believe me, I will do all I can to promote good feeling between us.'

She escorted him to where they were stashed away under a fallen branch, liberally masked by leaves. Leaving him to change into them, she moved back to the fire embers, intent upon brewing tea for her admirer.

★ ★ ★

Shortly after ten pm, Captain Chit located the last of Rondell's lookouts within a half mile of the upper end of the dump. He was told that after the earlier setback, the troops located on Nippon Hill had not ventured out. He was able to point out the actual location of the mules' corral, near the eastern tip of the dump, and give some detail about the distribution of guards.

Everton and the Blade brothers, who had once had charge of farm animals, moved around the top and slipped in behind the mules. A man who gave away his position near them by lighting a cigarette, died by a poisoned dart. A victim for Shan.

Chit accounted for a more alert guard with a thrown knife. Another came over when a figure wearing his partner's hat beckoned him closer. This third victim was strangled. The Bolis moved further down the slope and picked off three more, while the British did what they could to take stock of the different piles and crates in near darkness.

One or two of the commandos actually struck Japanese matches in an effort to make progress, but they did so wearing jockey caps in case anyone beyond their ken happened to notice anything suspicious. A full thirty minutes had dragged by with everybody feeling extreme tension before McCool and Chit jointly agreed that they had collected enough.

The eight mules played up in the loading, but as soon as they were clear of the trees and heading back towards the horseshoe camp they were no longer a match for the men of the mixed party. Captain Chit, himself, kept a few yards ahead, but all the others concentrated greatly upon the loaded beasts.

★ ★ ★

In a small shelter constructed out of fallen branches, split bamboos and leaves, the girl Shin stirred towards wakefulness as a distant scout tapped out a warning message on two short lengths of bamboo.

She moved an inch or two without wanting to come awake and rediscovered that she was in the arms of Scoop Britwell. She tapped him lightly on the chest with the tip of an index finger. He showed no sign of responding.

She murmured: 'Someone is coming.'

He asked her to say it again, but she was reluctant to destroy an idyllic moment. Earlier, they had had a conversation which had started with his querying her name, Shin. She had informed him that her full name was Shinbawnu, after a queen of her country. He had enquired whether she would have liked to be that queen. She had informed him 'no' because the queen had to share the king with other queens.

Later, he said he was pleased because she was not called after a portion of human anatomy. He had to explain where the shin was and that led to further exploration. He had finally fallen asleep while explaining that the scent of jasmine — blown across them by a gentle breeze — was sometimes called 'Queen of the Night'.

She chuckled as she remembered his love-talk, mildly slurred by rice wine used as warming medicine.

'Hey, hey, Britwell, someone is coming. Do you want them to find us like this? This is your Queen of the Night protesting!'

She playfully bit his ear and that helped to bring him back to wakefulness. Seconds later, he shouldered his way out of their love nest, grumbling bitterly.

★   ★   ★

Chit appeared out of the shadows. He lightly embraced the girl and gripped Britwell's hand, informing him that all had gone well.

'We pause for a rest here, drink tea, perhaps and then go on to the pagoda with our booty. Have you had any messages?'

'None at all,' Britwell informed him, and he moved away to greet those who were holding the mules in check.

★　★　★

The time was nearly four in the morning and the whole outfit admitted to having leaden legs by the time they toiled up the last of the slope to the pagoda, the historic shrine which for four hundred years had silhouetted the hill top against the sky line.

The Place of the Chins was a cold bleak spot for the end of the journey, but the further physical effort required to shift the mule-back stores into the secret chamber on the eastern side of the base counteracted some of the sharpness in the breeze at that altitude.

One more surprise came out of that night in the shape of a runner from the major in the village. Chit hurried to meet him, the fellow jerking out his message and attempting to restore his straining lungs at the same time. McCool and his men used the sudden arrival as an excuse to break off. They clustered around the captain and his fellow villager.

Chit explained. 'The major has much new information. Firstly, the road which you crossed to come to Daung Bazar has been undermined by diggers. But there is this other road to the east, not so good for traffic but passable.'

Chin pointed over his shoulder, beyond the pagoda.

'The Japs may come south by that road, in lorries. He thinks they will attack this pagoda, cross by the saddle and link up with other units at the railway. He says we must do all we can to divert, or stop altogether, the Jap lorry-borne infantry.'

McCool squatted between the forelegs of the nearest stone beast.

'Surely, 'e doesn't expect us to nip down there before breakfast and set up an ambush? Twelve ruddy men, short on sleep, an' that!'

Chit was withdrawn into himself,

thinking hard. Britwell was stretched out along the base of another animal figure, his shape not unlike the pose of the reclining Buddha in the building. His voice came from under his new coolie hat.

'I'd say he expects to get down there early and prepare the road before the Japs arrive with some of that loot we've been packing away. A few mines and such like. Eh, Chit?'

Chit chattered suddenly in full agreement while McCool cursed himself for not having seen what was so clear to their damned interfering civvy.

18

In the cold light of near dawn there was a lot of arguing between the fighting men before a plan was worked out. The first move to come out of the new instructions was the return of the messenger and the girl, Shin, to the village.

Britwell broke away from the discomfited commandos and embraced Shin after her brother. That night, the journalist had begun to have real feelings for the land of the pagodas. It had taken the company of the girl to make him see that Burma deserved to be held from the Japanese for its own sake, rather than just as a buffer between the enemy and India.

He stood beside Shan and watched the messenger and the girl go off down the slope in the direction of the village, each leading a mule laden with valuable stores. The parting told him that he had formed a real affection for the girl, and now he saw things differently.

Would Daung Bazar get a mauling from the Japanese for being too pro-British? Only time would tell.

As the trees swallowed the hurrying human figures and the two beasts he returned to the scene of the discussion and perceived that Ahmed and Yusuf had already loaded up two more beasts. Everton was standing by them with a cigar butt cupped in the palm of his hand.

'Are you going with the road squad, mate?'

'Sure, Scoop. Somebody 'as to show willin'. Why don't you come along as my partner? We might 'ave an easier time than the blokes left be'ind up 'ere.'

Britwell made up his mind quickly. 'All right, I'll speak to Chit. Give me a couple of minutes.'

Chit, who was thoroughly out of sympathy with McCool, saw Britwell's offer as a way out of his difficulty. He agreed with alacrity, and spent nearly five minutes describing the best portion of the valley floor track for placing the explosives. Everton listened closely, and the

Bolis and Shan translated Chit's words into Burmese for greater clarity among themselves.

Dawn was rumbling in the east as the party of five set off down the winding east slope below the pagoda. There were no signs of enemy activities in that area, which was a relief in the circumstances. Shan led the way, in spite of his weariness. The Bolis followed him, each in charge of a mule, while the British pair brought up the rear.

Britwell, who had a choice of clothing, kept on his khaki so that Everton would not feel like the odd man out. The animals proved more surefooted than the men, although they were handicapped by their loads.

Everton stumbled one time and fetched up rather shakily against the legs of Scoop, but the latter managed to retain his balance on the narrow precipitous path. Much lower down, a small boulder gave way under the journalist whose legs let him down. He was clinging to a protruding tree root when the stocky Merseysider rescued him.

The eastern sky was bright by the time they reached the bottom. The temperature was rising steadily and the pagoda above them was completely obscured by rolling mists hanging about the slopes of the ridge.

Some thirty feet above the track itself, the party halted and studied their immediate surroundings. Ahmed's sharp eyes spotted a ledge located slightly above them and some fifty yards away. A tree uprooted in the last monsoon had carried away a substantial portion of the slope. At its widest, the ledge was over twenty feet from front to back.

'It looks a likely place to use as a temporary base,' Britwell murmured.

Everton grunted his approval. The beasts were quickly manoeuvred onto it. They were restless at first, but when their loads were unpacked they settled down and partook of a long overdue rest.

Feeling rather guilty, the men squatted on the ledge. They drank and smoked and passed the binoculars from hand to hand, all of them being anxious not to be seen by the others. It was a little bit frightening being cut off from the heights by the mist.

They ate a snack of curried rice which had been kept lukewarm in some broad leaves. Next, they drank water and the two Britishers smoked. The total lack of any activity other than that of the usual jungle creatures got on their nerves.

Abruptly, after ten minutes, Everton sprang to his feet and paced up and down. He admitted to being nervous. His excellent senses gave him no cause for anxiety, but he was unable to rest properly with the mining job still ahead of them.

Shan, whose youth was beginning to catch up on him after the sleepless night, was left to guard the beasts and maintain a watch. The other four went off down the slope carrying four mines and some grenades, moving as quickly as their caution would allow them.

A breathless walk along the track, no more than thirty yards, brought them to a section of corduroy road. A piece which in the past had rapidly turned to mud at the first torrential downpour. Now, its surface was reinforced by light tree boles rigged across it.

Everton began to show his expertise. 'Scoop, mate, 'ow would it be if we make some adjustments to these logs? Put the mines under them in pairs like. An' maybe add a grenade or two for extra measure.'

'You're the expert,' Britwell opined. 'Which are we going to uproot?'

The stocky Liverpudlian made his choice and all four of them used their strength to extract the log. Underneath it, two mines were buried to the required depth. The same operation was repeated about twenty-five yards further along.

The Bolis employed their senses between lifts to keep a sharp lookout, which was just as well, because Everton was deeply immersed in his planning and Scoop was following his every move. Everton was rigging up grenade booby traps just off the track and wide of the mined areas when Ahmed snapped his fingers.

He called: 'The mist is clearing, Sahib

Everton. We can see the pagoda now.'

The information was acknowledged. The emergence of the Place of the Chins seemed to lift the spirits of the natives, but it did nothing for the other two. Everton had just straightened up and massaged his rounded shoulders (which would have kept him out of the army in peacetime) when the first of a series of bright flashes momentarily showed above the tree-clad slopes of the ridge towards the south.

The ground vibrated a little, preceding an explosion which seemed to be directly above them.

'Hell's bells,' Britwell yelled hoarsely, 'what's happening now?'

Everton rubbed his inward curving nose, spat into the dust, and uttered a couple of Merseyside oaths. 'It's the Japs, up on Nippon 'Ill. They've got artillery up there. I reckon we should 'ave reccied them a bit closer before now. They're firin' at the pagoda.'

Soil and small rocks cascaded down the upper slopes across which their path of descent zigzagged. Gathering together their equipment, they hurried away from the track side and made their way back to the ledge.

They found Shan startled into wakefulness. He was dancing up and down the ledge showing acute anxiety. About half a dozen shells by that time had landed, and at least one of them had hit stone work. He pointed up the slope as his friends arrived.

'They are shelling the pagoda, but the Chin Taes will protect it.'

The Bolis remained silent as they tried to read the outcome of the action. Everton and Britwell had no confidence in Shan's prophecy, but they kept their doubts to themselves. The shelling lasted for twenty minutes. For ten minutes more, they squatted with their senses alert, awaiting the landing of more projectiles, but nothing happened.

A feeling that their retreat had been cut off passed between them. After a protracted silence, Ahmed spoke of the future.

'Sahib Britwell, what should we do now?'

'As we don't know what has happened up there, I think we should stay on this ledge and await developments. If Chit has other plans for us he can send a messenger. If enemy lorries appear, we shall not be seen directly, and we may be able to harass the convoy before we withdraw.'

The strength of his argument was at once approved by the others. Shan agreed to stay awake, and this was a signal for the four saboteurs to select a suitable spot and stretch out in sleep. All of them were enjoying an exhausted slumber by the time the lad had rigged palm fronds in the vertical rear wall of the ledge to keep the sun off them.

★　★　★

'*Sahib Britwell, Sahib Everton, wake up! Please!*'

Shan was shaking the two Englishmen by the shoulder as though they were in serious trouble. Ahmed and Yusuf were already awake and giving their attention to the slope a little further north.

Everton muttered: 'Bloody hell, what's 'appenin' now?'

'What is it, Shan?' Britwell demanded brusquely, from a kneeling position.

'There are many people coming down the slope towards us, sahib. If they came round the end of the ridge, it could be the Japanese, or people from our village. Something is happening. We must be on the alert.'

One after another, the five men scrambled off the ledge and threw themselves down in the bunched grass north of their rest camp. Everton was checking over a Sten gun and Britwell going over a rifle with a wolfish grin on his face.

The Bolis crept forward, ready with their *dahs*. Three minutes later, they were back again, reporting that it was the villagers on the move. The major had decided that it was time for them to evacuate Daung Bazar and seek another location for their village before the Japs came along in force.

Britwell caught at his breath. He had heard rumours about the way in which the Japanese served villages known to be

278

pro-British. The old people might be killed, the women raped and the able-bodied men taken in with the railroad building task force.

'We must make sure they don't cross the road near the booby traps!'

Shan and the Bolis made off to lead the villagers down the easiest part of the slope, while the Englishmen took charge of the protesting mules and moved them down to the lower level. The latter pair waited on the track twenty yards clear of the mines and grenades. Up above them the short foliage was bright with moving *lungyis* and colourful blouses.

Britwell raised his glasses. There were scores of people on the move. Children in arms, walking toddlers, old ladies with wrinkled faces and troubled eyes. Elderly men with inches of white beard, and younger men bunched against their own kin, swinging their *dahs* and occasionally slashing away spiked shrubs.

Britwell had eyes for only certain people. Shin, Mashraf and the major. Of John Peel, there was no sign. Two women with well-rounded stomachs sat the backs of two mules taken along to the village by Shin and the messenger. Tiny children shared the ride.

No signs of Chit, or any of the commandos. Ahmed and Yusuf, looking troubled, led the procession across the track into the trees on the other side. Britwell grew tired of looking for Shin among the young women with white flowers in their hair. He thought that everyone in the party would read his thoughts without difficulty. Everton insisted that a pair of elderly sisters should ride the back of his mule, and Britwell forced himself to assist them onto the broad back.

Their bundles and those of others who were heavily laden were hastily secured to the back of the second mule. The messenger of the night before stepped out of the crowd and accepted the responsibility for leading it. Britwell's heart thumped.

'Where is Shin? Did she get back to the village all right?'

The enquiry chased the serious expression off the man's face. He pointed to the tail end of the procession and watched the Englishman hurry off in that direction. Mashraf was at the very end of the line, stumbling along with his customary dignity, and availing himself of the supporting arm of his grand-daughter, Shin.

The old man pushed Shin away from him as Britwell raced to their side. Scoop put his arm around the girl's shoulders and briefly clasped her in a bear hug. There were slight smudges under her bright eyes, sure signs that she had missed a lot of sleep and rest.

She said: 'Grandfather, the Sahib Britwell is a true friend of the Burmese.'

Britwell blushed under his newly acquired tan. He removed his sun spectacles and forced himself to be polite to the old man, while Shan embraced his sister and rapidly brought her up to date with a series of highly imaginative descriptive sentences in his native dialect.

'Tell me, Mashraf, are the Japanese close behind you?'

'No, Sahib Britwell, I do not think so. But the major says it is time to move on, and we trust his judgement. A Burmese village is soon constructed. There are many willing hands. You will be as welcome as before.'

Britwell nodded. He had a feeling that circumstances were beginning to work against him. 'Mashraf, I think your grandson, Shan, should go along with you and his sister. He is tired, and very young to do the dangerous work of a man.'

Mashraf approved, and Britwell turned to Shan and repeated what he had said to the old man. The old man said: 'Sahib Britwell speaks with wisdom. Soon there will be many British in the district. There must be young people of my own family to make them welcome.'

The headman shook hands with Scoop and tactfully moved off across the track, leaving the young people to say their farewells.

Britwell said: 'Shan, your sister has become very dear to me. Don't let anything happen to her. If I get the opportunity, I will follow you.'

He kissed the girl, put her hand into that of her brother, and urged them into the trees. His eyes strained after them, although all his instincts were for getting them away with all haste from this potential theatre of danger. Ahmed and Yusuf came back while he was still staring into the trees which had absorbed the brother and sister.

A few yards up the track, Everton, who had witnessed the last exchanges, pretended to be trying his hand at rolling a cigar.

* * *

The peculiar sounds of flying shells came from the north about ten minutes later. By that time, the Bolis, Everton and Britwell had scrambled back to their ledge and given themselves over to a session of vigilance. They had already concluded that Chit and his commando force had left the pagoda on a mission or, alternatively, made a strategic withdrawal.

Although they had been expecting some show of force from the north, the sudden falling of shells into the trees which had so recently absorbed the villagers momentarily stupefied them.

Ahmed and Yusuf gripped each other and registered fear for their kin.

Everton reeled off three of his best foul oaths while Britwell stood like a man transfixed, hearing the shattering explosions and the rending crash of falling trees.

'Lorry borne field guns, that's what they must be,' the Merseysider opined. 'But what are they shootin' at? I reckon something's balked them on the road an' they're just firin' for pure devilment. One thing we do know, though, the bastards certainly mean business, an' that's for sure!'

Another salvo landed across the track, and Britwell was about to bawl out his partner for not showing concern for the villagers when Everton leapt down off the ledge and started for the track. A rogue shell came whining towards them. The trio on the ledge belatedly threw themselves flat. The projectile ripped into the hillside below them throwing rocks and stones in all directions.

When they looked up, there was a new crater and a small landslide building up on the spot where Everton had been. As one man, they dropped down to search for him, disregarding any further danger. They clawed and probed around the edges for two or three minutes without discovering any signs of the redoubtable commando.

Torn between two courses of action, Britwell urged the Bolis to keep on searching while he, himself, ran recklessly down the slope, across the track and into the trees. Perspiration was coursing down his face and he was getting the idea that he might never find the route taken by the villagers when he heard his name called.

'Sahib Britwell!'

He had never heard Shin's voice raised, nor any semblance of fear upon her lips.

'*Breetwell!*'

He changed direction to find the source of her voice.

'*Scoop!*'

Pressing anguish distorted her excellent English as he dodged the dusty craters and the trees suddenly bereft of animal life by the explosions. He found her on her knees, crouched over Shan whose body was pinned down by the branch of a fallen teak bole.

19

Shan's eyes were closed and his youthful face showed signs of pain. Britwell's thoughts were brusquely turned back to that other occasion when the wounded paratrooper had been carried along for so many miles and then killed at the river crossing. He thought that in this type of war the odds were always against casualties.

He knelt beside the girl and gripped her hands so hard that tears came to her eyes.

'His leg. His leg is broken, above the knee. The others have hurried on ahead. They are most fearful of shells and bombs. We cannot expect help from them. It would not be fair.'

'It's *my* fault, Shin,' Britwell murmured, his voice hoarse with anguish. 'I shouldn't have kept you back. But I'm sure we can help him.'

He tried to shift the pinning tree

branch himself, but all the weight of the massive tree seemed to be loaded against him. He stood up, conscious of failure in front of the girl and gasping as if the air he breathed was molten.

'The Bolis, I'll get the Bolis with their *dahs*.'

'They are all right? The last shell fell near where you must have been.'

She had noted the anguish in his face as soon as he arrived. He nodded. 'Ahmed and Yusuf are okay. But not Everton. He was scrambling down the slope to come over this side when the shell landed. He was buried. I must go.'

He gave her an agonized look, and ran back over the same route. She came a little way away from the fallen tree, so as to be able to point the way when he returned. At the track, he was breathless again. One glance was sufficient to show that Everton had not been unearthed. The Bolis were straining every effort to no avail, with soil up their brown arms to the biceps.

'Any luck?' he called up to them.

They both shook their hands and he

waved for them to join him.

'Bring all the spare gear! Shan has been injured by a falling tree!'

Again, the blind determined positive response from the redoubtable Bolis. They joined him almost at once and plunged into the trees, while further shells sailed across the sky, unseen but heard, to land — ludicrously enough — around the other salient point, Nippon Hill.

Between them, Britwell, Shin and Ahmed took the pressure off the leg by lifting the branch. Yusuf, an acknowledged master with the *dah*, deftly severed the branch. Shan was gently hauled clear. Tears coursed down Shin's face as she assisted Britwell with the splinting of the leg. At the same time, the Bolis prepared a stretcher.

Shan was laid upon the litter and ready to be moved off. They had just decided to take him up to the pagoda rather than attempt to rejoin the villagers when the sounds of approaching vehicles thwarted their plans. Hastily, they removed the injured youth into protective concealment.

The three men were watching from a safe distance when the Jap vehicles from the north began to use the mined track. First in line was a staff car with four men in it. To their surprise it negotiated the first mined spot and bumped along towards the second.

The shelling had stopped. The whining of lorry engines was strong and growing louder. The observers shared their attention between the staff car and the troop lorry which followed. Just when it seemed that neither vehicle was going to suffer there was a giant twin explosion.

The staff car sailed upwards in a tangled wreck of metal, its occupants all killed instantly. At the same time, the open-backed lorry was bounced and buckled in the heart of a blinding sheet of explosion tinged with orange and red flame. Greenclad infantrymen were hurled in all directions. Cries of anguish were drowned.

A man who fell heavily clear of the tailgate sprinted for the trees only to lose his life when a grenade went off. General consternation. Flames around the lorry's engine. Dust and splintered timber seemed to be everywhere.

An NCO from one of the field gun carriers further back came forward and tried to get some order out of the chaos. The trio of observers felt no sense of triumph. They eyed each other apprehensively from time to time and wondered what the outcome would be.

Presently, orders were shouted. Infantry on foot began to creep along the track looking for survivors. A way was found into the trees on the east side which was not so obvious. Two score of soldiers, fully armed, some on bicycles and carrying dismantled weapons, made a detour.

Time dragged ominously. Stretcher bearers went about their work, carrying the wounded to the rear. The cyclists and walking infantry had gone out of sight along the track towards the south. Ahmed crawled further north and came back to report that the Japanese were taking a break. All their personnel had withdrawn to the rear. The whole party clustered around the injured youth.

'He needs pain-killing tablets and expert attention,' Britwell murmured, 'otherwise I would suggest taking him further east to join up with the villagers. If we cross the track again and make for the pagoda we shall be taking an awful chance.'

Shin nodded. Britwell was able to read the near-inscrutable faces of the Bolis sufficiently well to know that they would take such a chance. While they squatted, pondering over the situation, they heard aircraft approaching. The area was becoming more and more significant as a war zone.

Britwell missed the sharp senses of Everton, as the planes flew in from the north. He recollected with a sharp pang of regret that he did not even know if Everton was the soldier's real name . . .

A curious Jap NCO was wandering further into the bush eating fruit when the first flight of British fighter-bombers approached. The sound of their engines made him turn about when he was too close to their hideout for comfort. Ahmed paused with his *dah* raised for a throw.

The fellow walked away again, still eating. Inadvertently, he had saved his own life.

In much the same way as the railhead had been attacked, a trio of planes flew down over the lorries and scattered their personnel with cannon fire. There was a big explosion as a petrol tank blew up, but one of the lorry-borne guns at least got off a few shells while the angle was right.

Off went the fighters, looking for other targets. Another, larger group with a different engine sound came in from the east. Bombers. More British markings. At a much higher altitude in the blue innocent sky, the bombers headed directly for Nippon Hill, releasing their bombs to fall like tiny silver pellets on the Jap strongpoint. Gun emplacements and machine-gun nests erupted, giving clear indication of the bombers' accuracy.

Lean, high-angled guns from somewhere by the dump and the railhead probed for them without scoring any hits. The bombers maintained course, and soon a second salvo was falling nose over tail towards the dump and the railhead.

The earth-shaking *crump* of explosions marked the progress of the raid to the combatants east of the ridge. The fighters flew over again, harassing Nippon Hill and the holed-up convoy from the north. And then came the third formation, this time from the north-east. Britwell had seen enough of them on the ground at Lalaghat to know they were troop carriers. Spewers of parachuted airborne troops. Headed, no doubt, for a cleared area south-west of the railhead where an airstrip could be established.

The troop transports came in threes, their progress marked by the grey puffs of exploding shells from the one lorry-borne gun in action.

'Why don't we go now, sahib, while everyone is looking into the sky?'

Shin's simple breathtaking logic surprised Britwell. He looked around for support, assured himself that he had it and gave his assent. At once the Bolis took up the litter, working as a team, as determined as ever. The enormous risk which they were about to take appalled the journalist, especially when he glanced down at the fragile girl and thought what her loss would mean to him.

In the event of their being apprehended they could expect no quarter: not after the wholesale destruction caused by the mining of the track. Shin straightened herself up to her full height as the foliage thinned out before them. She stared up at the tiny bit of roof just visible at the Place of the Chins, smiled briefly and headed for the track.

She was about to lead them over. A rifle lay alongside of the semi-conscious youth. Britwell was a yard or so to the rear, armed with a Sten which Everton had brought with him. Some thirty yards from the nearest crater, she paused, hidden from the north only by a single *bizat* bush. Shan groaned. Ahmed licked his dry lips. Yusuf adjusted his hold on the litter as his brother stopped.

Britwell offered up a silent prayer. Shin started off again, a diminutive coolie figure in a flattened conical bamboo hat. The Bolis moved onto the track, their feet as sure as if they were trained balancers doing an act. Britwell followed with a dry throat, abjectly conscious of his Jap jockey cap. Should he have been wearing the coolie hat made for him by Shin?

His stomach rumbled with fear for his party. The last flight of troop carriers disappeared over the lowest part of the saddle as Shin reached the other side and started to climb. The Japs whose attention had been riveted to the skies would look around now. Their minds would be sharpened by thoughts of aggression and vengeance.

The corpses were still lying about, compelling Britwell's brief attention as he surveyed the scene of terrible destruction. He started up the opposite slope as his troubled thoughts prompted him to study Everton's mound before it was too late. Perspiration was starting out of his forehead and the nape of his neck as his rubber shoes slipped on soil loosened earlier. He came near to losing his balance and falling against Yusuf's legs.

That would never do. Fifty yards would see them into useful concealing scrub, but that fifty yards could not be hurried. Any stumbling might lead to disaster. This day, he reflected, would go down in his memory as the longest of his life. Extreme tension constricted his breathing. Yard by yard, Shin led them towards cover.

The sky noises faded towards the south-west. His buzzing ears began to pick out once again the gentler sounds of nature. Far above him, a pair of green pigeons hedge-hopped a clump of bamboos and pursued one another from a banana tree to a coconut palm.

He thought: Nature is normal. Man is the only animal who is truly wild. Man is the beast.

He felt an uncontrollable desire to turn around and blast the area from which the Japs might appear with automatic fire. He wanted to shout and yell his new philosophy to the skies, but Yusuf muttered something in his native tongue and that broke the tension.

They achieved cover and went on for another thirty yards. At that point, with the binoculars flapping against his chest, Britwell paused. He was determined to take a last look at Everton's mound before altitude made it impossible. Where was the camera? He had lost track of it in the last day or so. He went over in his mind the casualties which had occured since the glider's abortive landing. The American sergeant pilot, Sandy Malone. Ronnie Peyton, the photographer, who wanted to get into action and take pictures. Vallance, the parachutist, who had survived his first setback only to die a soldier's death at the river crossing. Ginger More, whose weakness for liquor had betrayed him. Douty and Smith, and now Everton, a soldier's soldier: a man for all critical occasions.

He dropped back a yard or two and focused the glasses down the slope below the ridge. The mound of soil had a fresh look about it. He had a feeling that it would remain undisturbed for a long time: become a part of the ridge which supported the Place of the Chins.

A distant flash of light made him blink. A bullet ricochetted off a rock surface below him and he felt a slight blow on his right side. He sank down and his senses swam. The echo of the sniper's shot was fading when Shin crouched beside him, closely followed by the Bolis.

Ahmed pulled his shirt away. 'It is a flesh wound, but it may have hit a rib. We must patch him up and take him with us. I don't see any sign of the sniper, or anyone interested in our whereabouts.'

He answered to their talk like a man in a daze. His breathing was laboured, but his legs still functioned. They patched him and the girl took him by the hand, leading and hauling him up the slope. For a long time he was only conscious of certain small noises. His own stertorous breathing and the panting of Shin.

Some time later, he was mildly conscious of being no longer in motion. He was on his back on a comfortable litter in a chamber which he vaguely identified as the pagoda. A fine net mosquito screen hung above him with a white flower pinned to it.

He could not move his right arm which seemed to be bandaged across his chest, but that did not seem to matter. The flower made him feel good. Only one thing prevented him from slipping off into a deep sleep. He felt cold. He murmured as much.

A slight familiar figure lifted the net and put a cup to his lips. When he had slaked his thirst, she crept in beside him and the soft contours of her body slowly lifted his temperature. He put his left arm about her and nodded as the lips touching his ear told him he was safe.

20

Although he was running a slight temperature, Britwell slept. Shin's closeness gave him comfort. About two hours later, the girl slipped out from under the net without disturbing him.

The shadows were lengthening in the chamber of the Buddha when a bout of spasmodic shooting developed in the direction of Nippon Hill. A particularly sharp crack roused the sleeping journalist. He turned uneasily and looked about him.

Shin was kneeling a few yards away with his note pad resting on the base of the great reclining statue. She was concentrating hard on the notes she was writing about the events of the previous night and that day. She had guessed correctly that he would want a record of what had been happening recently, and that he would be troubled, not having the use of his right hand.

He smiled in her direction, and wondered who had given her sufficient education to write in English. She glanced in his direction from time to time, her broad brow furrowed and the tip of her tongue exploring her lips.

He called for a drink after dozing for about half an hour. Shin nodded. She read through what she had written and decided that it would suffice. He sipped the wine she brought and held the hand which supported the cup, not wanting her to leave him.

Her eyelids were heavy through weariness again. She needed little persuasion to curl up beside him again and close her eyes.

Major Rondell arrived about eight o'clock. He stood over the litter and regarded the couple sharing it. Shin was sound asleep. Britwell winked at him and he came round to kneel beside him.

'Hard luck, old man,' he murmured. 'The Bolis tell me you have a bullet groove above the waist. The shell glanced off a rib, which is probably broken and there is a chance the rib touched a lung.

You'll need careful handling for a while, but there's no need for you to worry over it.'

'How are things going, major?'

'I'll be able to tell you in an hour or so, but I have reason to think all's well with your mates. The RAF bombing job appeared to be very effective and I have great hopes about the landing in force to make an airstrip. So get some rest if you can. Do you want a sleeping tablet?'

'No. No, thanks. I'm too curious about the latest developments to want to sleep at this time. If you have any pressing jobs, don't let me keep you.'

Rondell nodded and grinned. 'I thought I'd just take five minutes off, long enough to read what Shin has been writing for you, and then there'll be chores. Any special developments, I'll let me know.'

John Peel rose to his feet, crossed to where the pad was lying and moved with it to an opening high in the wall. He pursed his lips, pushed back his cap and started to read. He found Shin's work compulsive reading. She had gone into great detail about the previous night, and all the events of that day up to the time when sleep dampened her ardour.

As he read, the major sensed how much love and affection the writer felt for the wounded Englishman. He glanced from one to the other, marvelled a little over them and reread some of the more touching paragraphs. When he had finished, he sighed, laid his jockey cap on the paper and paced up and down for a while, barefooted. He perceived that Britwell's temperature was up, that he was rambling a little and reflected that the correspondent was incident prone.

He had heard of his penchant for being at the core of the action long before Britwell appeared in Burma, and he hoped that the fellow would live to send many more inspired despatches from the front.

Meanwhile, Scoop's eyes were half-closed, but his ears were missing nothing. His fever seemed to have heightened his powers of hearing. The Bolis tiptoed in shortly afterwards and reported that men on foot were approaching.

Charges had been placed at the bases

of the macabre Chin figures: charges which would only be fired if the worst came to the worst.

A few pregnant minutes went by before the tension went out of the building. Captain Chit was returning from Nippon Hill. In they came looking tired, weary and mauled, but triumphant. Sergeant McCool had been killed in the last of the hand to hand fighting on the Hill, during the assault after the bombing. The commandos were reduced to Corporal Judd and six others.

To Britwell, Rondell's voice appeared to boom as he explained how they had planned to blast the Chin Taes and the surrounding earth, if the Japs happened to come first. Now, it was not necessary.

Judd and the others quietly moved around to shake Britwell's hand, but when they found his left arm occupied they contented themselves by murmuring a greeting and patting him on the head.

There was a doubt in Chit's voice when he mentioned the demolition charges left by his men on Nippon Hill, but the despondency left the decimated group as the first of a long series of charges began to wreak havoc among the Japanese gun emplacements and machine-gun nests. Britwell heard their subdued joyful talk, dozed a little and revived when a tired Burmese messenger arrived from the south-west.

Rondell translated for the benefit of the British. 'The airstrip is established. I am to report there personally, taking with me any British commando personnel. So the news is good.'

Another Burmese, left as a lookout beyond the saddle, also brought cheering news. The tip of Nippon Hill was no more. The charges had flattened it, and at the same time created a landslide which had seriously handicapped and thwarted troops climbing the ridge towards it from the lorry convoy.

Night closed in. Lookouts were posted. All who could, slept.

* * *

In brilliant sunshine half a day later, Britwell awoke on his bobbing litter to find himself part of a procession proceed-ing down hill. The fever had left him. His head was clear. He stared about him, full of curiosity. Further down the slope two Burmese were carrying the litter which held Shan.

Britwell's stretcher was in the capable hands of the Bolis. The familiar earrings and broad back of Ahmed were at the front end. A backward overhead glance brought a bright smile from the homely scarred face of Yusuf, who chuckled with pleasure in spite of the weight he was carrying. Corporal Judd and his men were bringing up the rear while Captain Chit and Major Rondell did the leading.

Shin, clad once again in her green skirt and pale blouse, paced easily along beside him, toying with the strap of her coolie hat.

For a minute or two, Scoop idly watched the tantalizing swing of her shapely posterior in the sheath-like skirt, and then he reached for his note pad which had been tucked under his hip by some thoughtful person.

He noted that she had given up the

habit of wearing the white flower, and that his shirt had a fresh blossom in it. With a conscious effort he removed his gaze from her and started to read what she had written.

KILL PETROSINO!

Frederick Nolan

It is the turn of the century. Lieutenant Joe Petrosino of the New York Police Department is a man with an obsession. Believing that there is a secret society controlling organised crime in America, he aims to expose the Mafia. With disbelieving superiors, he alone must face the feared Don Vito Cascio Ferro. Would-be informers are too scared to talk, but Petrosino gets his first lead with the discovery of a brutally murdered body in a New York alley . . .

FEAR OF STRANGERS

E. C. Tubb

Instead of the welcome they'd expected, the returning crew of the first interstellar spaceship were kept in space, imprisoned in their craft — in quarantine, as carriers of a deadly alien disease! When the prisoners escaped, the worried authorities hired Earth's top detective Martin Slade to track them down, little suspecting that Slade had his own personal agenda. Slade's search for the missing crew spans millions of miles of space, following a trail of hideous deaths . . .

THE TORMENT OF SHERLOCK HOLMES

Val Andrews

Holmes has fallen into a state of deep depression, and Watson is trying his best to help. Whilst walking through Regent's Park, Watson witnesses a heavily veiled woman drop a ticket for property lodged at Victoria Station. Unable to return the ticket to her, Watson claims the property and appeals to Holmes to trace the owner, hoping that the stimulation of a fresh investigation will rouse his companion. But the item, a large hat box, turns out to hold some rather gruesome contents . . .

THE RATTENBURY MYSTERY

John Russell Fearn

When the infamous theatrical agent Amos Rattenbury is found stabbed to death in his London office, the weight of suspicion falls on Dorene Grey, a young actress. Assistant Commissioner, Sir Digby Hilton of Scotland Yard, is assigned to find the missing Dorene. However, she has two champions: Sir Digby's brother Terry, and the mysterious figure known as 'The Phantom of the Films'. And she will need their help to escape the fate planned for her by a cunning murderer.

MR. WALKER WANTS TO KNOW

Ernest Dudley

Mr. Walker, the Cockney rag and bone man, is always bumping into other people's troubles. After the murder of old Cartwright in the jeweller's shop, he becomes involved in adventures with his friend Inspector Wedge of Scotland Yard, with the arrest of a crooked police officer, and the escape of Cartwright's killer. Then there is another death — in Mr. Walker's own sitting room — but his problems are just beginning, as he discovers that he himself is a candidate for murder!

SCORPION: SECOND GENERATION

Michael R. Linaker

The colony of deadly scorpions at Long Point Nuclear Plant was eradicated. Or so people thought . . . Over a year later, entomologist Miles Ranleigh receives a worrying telephone call. A man has been fatally poisoned by toxic venom, identical to the Long Point scorpions' — but far more powerful. Miles and his companion Jill Ansty must race to destroy the fresh infestation. But this is a new strain of scorpion. Mutated and irradiated, they're larger, more savage — and infected with a deadly virus fatal to humans. And they're breeding . . .